THE RAVENWOOD CURSE

By
W. A. Holmes

For information, or to order additional copies, please contact:

Beacon Publishing Group
P.O. Box 41573 Charleston, S.C. 29423
800.817.8480 | beaconpublishinggroup.com

Publishers catalog available by request.

ISBN-13: 978-1-949472-57-8
ISBN-10: 1-949472-57-8

Published in 2023. New York, NY 10001.

First Edition. Printed in the USA.

THE RAVENWOOD CURSE

Table of Contents

THE RAVENWOOD CURSE

By

W. A. Holmes

Chapter 1

The wind has shifted. From beyond the woods in the west, it now heads eastward towards Visitation Lake. A rare occurrence, but its frequency may be on the rise. The first time came only three months ago when an evil rose up intent on destroying Angel Falls. Thus the saying among residents of Angel Falls, "An ill wind blows from the west." All might have been lost, had an equally powerful force not acted in time to stop it.

Heroes can take many forms. They can teach, be uniformed protectors of the public, work as health professionals, give to charities or perform volunteer work—among other things. Then there are those who, because of an extraordinary birth, one day find themselves forced into the spotlight through no desire of their own. Having won this recent battle with the supernatural, Justin Thyme, a true hero, now craves a return to some of life's quieter, simpler moments.

Sitting patiently on the couch in the family's living room, Justin watches, emotionless, as his dad, Dr. Mark Thyme, analyzes the outline of a human form on his laptop screen. The software allows him to control, register, and reprogram nanobots active inside Justin. Nanobots were injected into the preemie infant Justin to save his life. Under normal circumstances, these nanobots would have dissipated from his body three months after their introduction into Justin's system. However, the form on the computer screen clearly indicated they were as numerous and active as ever. The best guess Dr. Thyme could offer for their longevity was the existence of a symbiotic relationship between the nanobots and Justin's unique genetic makeup. The angelic part of him was keeping the nanobots alive.

The aforementioned evil, sensing the powers that would one day develop in Justin, actively pursued the abortion of Justin when he was yet unborn. Betrayed by a nurse having a change of conscience, the aborted, premature child was taken to Dr. Thyme whose nanotechnology saved him. That technology had been specifically designed to aid preemies in their continued development. Thus was the boy saved and later adopted by Dr. Thyme and his wife Jean.

The Nephilim gene, discovered when Justin turned eighteen, altered his skin, making it a pliable, impenetrable outer covering. The best description of his skin at the molecular level would be to compare it to a knight's chainmail garment. Quantifying the condition of the nanobots required using the computer program because a normal hypodermic needle could no longer penetrate the boy's skin in order to obtain blood needed for such an examination.

Of his other bodily functions, everything complied to Justin's "new normal." The nanobots, and possibly to a degree his angelic genes, allowed Justin to hold his breath under water for fifteen minutes! Under duress, Justin's new nature made it possible for him to move with incredible speed over short distances. This was demonstrated when he saved Beverly Heartstone from being killed by Dr. Siffer a few months ago.

Justin's body can take a beating, having bones now as strong and lightweight as titanium. And with the ability to get inside people's heads, Justin finds ways into places inaccessible by ordinary human beings.

"Are you almost done?" Justin asked.

His dad's fingers tickled the keyboard. "Hold still, son—almost."

"Every time we do this I'm afraid you'll find something weird!" Justin complained. "I just wish I could be normal!"

Justin's dad finished entering information into the laptop and closed it. He removed the stethoscope from his ears. "I know, son. I wish I could help you, but normalcy aside, everything looks good here."

"I keep looking over my shoulders to see if I've sprouted wings—or worse!" Justin said. "How embarrassing would that be—or horns!"

His dad replaced the stethoscope into a medical bag. "Horns belong to the devil. You're no devil, believe me!"

"Or a tail! What if I grow a tail?"

His dad tried to suppress a laugh. "As far as I know, angels don't have tails! But while we're on the subject, have you experienced any new visions or new abilities?"

"Thankfully, no!" Justin said. "Things have been nice and dull, so far."

"Well, keep me informed," his dad said, trying to remain optimistic. He could not bring himself to express his concern that Justin's transformation may not yet be fully realized. Only a few short months had passed since his son's eighteenth birthday when these abilities first appeared.

Time to change the subject. "By the way, how's Beverly feeling?" his dad asked.

"Her leg is completely healed—which reminds me! I have some photos I need to drop off to her today!"

Dr. Thyme placed his laptop inside its carrying case. "What's the subject?"

"Birds—of all the things!" Justin answered, appreciating the change in subject. "The Tribune is doing a piece on birds of our area. She asked me to do some bird watching. I snapped all twenty birds on her list plus a few she didn't have."

"We have more than twenty kinds of birds in Angel Falls, don't we?" Justin's dad asked.

"Not so much. Drive a few dozen miles west of here, past the mountains, and you'll find more. I did some research to get into the spirit of the assignment," Justin said. "It'll all be part of the anniversary edition of the Tribune coming out before Christmas."

"Well, we're done here. You'd better not keep your editor waiting—say hello for me."

The Falls Tribune was preparing to publish an Angel Falls Anniversary Edition of the newspaper. With most people today history holds little interest. Whether native born or imported from out of state, a town's history rarely enters into its residents' conversations. Even the remarkable history of Angel Falls has been relegated to something of a legend, mostly forgotten.

Justin's very existence is irrevocably tied to that history. Over the centuries since its founding, a wandering gene appeared in certain individuals at different times in the life of the town. The gene's origin: the son of an angel and a human, a Nephilim. Beginning with those angels who saved the dying town hundreds of years ago when it was called Grangeville, to the Nephilim heir, to an episodic individual appearing intermittently throughout the following decades, Angel Falls has been kept safe. Now Justin's turn—by the 'luck of the draw' had come.

Of course, you can bet wherever supernatural forces for good abide, attacks from evil forces will not be far away. Such has been Justin's existence, from the attempt to abort him before he was born, to an attack on the town of Angel Falls itself. None are exempt. It's as if this angelic existence made Angle Falls a magnet for less than desirable elements. In one sense, the very thing once responsible for saving the town had also cursed it. Of course, the opposite could be true: through foreknowledge of future attacks the Sovereign One always made certain to have in place a warrior suited to the task of deliverance.

Now, high atop the plateau west of town, the wind-rippled surface of Visitation Lake stirred under a sudden change in the wind's direction. Once again, the ill wind blows.

A once popular TV show's announcer would present some poor soul who was "about to enter The

Twilight Zone." Besides his family, only Justin's two friends know of his special powers, and how potential dangers 'lurk around every corner'. That's how Justin's more apprehensive friend, Charles Philip Underwood, also known as CPU, looks at it. He assisted Justin in stopping Doctor Louis Siffer, bent on destroying Angel Falls. Derrick Cartwright, Justin's other good friend, became caught in Siffer's trap. These three were about to find themselves inevitably drawn into another Twilight Zone of their own.

****

New Horizons Retirement Community peacefully rests on one hundred acres of prime real estate, offering a choice of living quarters for both single individuals and married couples over fifty-five. Jeb Wechsler, seventy-five, chose the cottage style dwelling over the apartments offered by New Horizons. His current living quarters were originally a sample cottage. As the population of New Horizons grew, new cottages sprang up on newly acquired land. Wechsler jumped on the original sample cottage when it was offered for sale. His reason: the newly constructed cottages were too tightly clustered for his comfort. It did not please him to have neighbors sitting right on top of him.

Wechsler entertained a visitor today from Hi Tech Computer Sales, a local computer retail outfit. CPU, the owner's son, came up with an idea to visit New Horizons one Saturday each month to address any resident's computer complaints. The successful plan brought in several new customers to Hi Tech who would otherwise never have known the computer outlet existed. It also helped those residents who were unable to leave their homes to travel the distance to Hi Tech. CPU found himself scheduling about seven or eight residents per month making for a full Saturday. It was a win-win setup.

Wechsler's cottage was sparsely furnished. CPU noticed some furniture covered in plastic. Ornamental doilies decorated the end tables by the couch and the dining room table. Tassels adorned the bottom edge of some of the lampshades. The apartment's furnishings reminded him of his great grandfather's apartment when he was alive. This man, however, was only fifteen years older than his dad.

A push-button phone hung on the kitchen wall with the only electronic device in the cottage being Wechsler's laptop. He did not own a cell phone or television. Several bookcases lined with dozens of volumes told CPU that Mr. Wechsler was an avid reader.

"You gonna make it so I can Face-time my brother overseas?" Wechsler asked.

"That is the plan, sir," CPU answered. He opened Wechsler's laptop and turned it on. He wondered why Wechsler, electronics-shy as he was, even cared to own a laptop. Now he understood.

"That contraption is way slow, by the way," Wechsler continued. "Speed it up, will ya?"

"I shall do my best."

CPU concentrated on the laptop now running on the kitchen table in front of him. His elbows straddled the laptop as his hands cradled his head, massaging it. It was something he did when working out a particularly unusual problem. After several minutes he realized the laptop recognized Wechsler's Wi-Fi signal, but for some reason failed to connect to the Internet.

On a hunch, CPU checked the antivirus software. He noticed it was not getting regular, automatic updates. When his attempt to manually update the software also failed he made the bold move to uninstall it altogether. When doing this also failed to revive the Wi-Fi connection he knew what he had to do.

Reaching into his toolkit, CPU pulled out a flash drive and inserted it into one of the USB ports. He ran a utility designed to completely removed any remnants of the antivirus software. Once the utility finished the Internet connection returned successfully, but the computer still acted sluggish. He installed a fresh, new copy of an updated version of the antivirus software, restarted the laptop and tested the Internet. The Internet still worked, yet with each mouse click the laptop chugged along even slower.

"I am going to run a full virus scan now, Mr. Wechsler," CPU said.

After twenty minutes Wechsler asked, "How many lifetime's this gonna take? I need to be someplace."

"Not much longer—it has to complete the scan to be effective," CPU said.

After another ten minutes a total of twenty viruses were found and deleted. The computer restarted once more. When it completed booting up the improvement in speed was clearly noticeable.

CPU returned the flash drive to his toolkit. "Your antivirus program crashed. I fixed it and removed some viruses. You are good to go!"

Concerned, Wechsler asked, "Is that why the darn thing was so clunky?"

"Absolutely. But you are all fixed now. I updated the Operating System too."

Wechsler went to his desk and took out his checkbook. "So how much you takin' me for?" he asked.

"Um, make it out to Hi Tech for fifty dollars, please."

"I'll never get these computers—a necessary evil I suppose," Wechsler said. He signed the check and handed it to CPU. "You all done for the day?"

CPU closed up the toolkit. "Here, yes. A guy from school needs help setting up email on his new phone—then I am off until next month."

Wechsler became a bit anxious as CPU rose to leave. "Turn that gizmo off, would ya?" he said. "And I always close the lid! I don't want nobody spying on me through the camera!"

"You can put a piece of dark electric tape over the camera, Mr. Wechsler."

"Nah. Just close it. Then nobody can hear me either!"

CPU smiled. He thought how silly to be concerned about such a thing. But he complied with the old man's wishes, turned the laptop off and closed the lid. He then proceeded to the front door. As he started to open the door Wechsler quickly reached out and pushed it shut.

Keeping his hand on the door, Wechsler looked intently at CPU. "Just one more thing, kid. You're smart; keep your eyes open. Something ain't right around this place!"

Chapter 2

Ravenwood Estate, abandoned in the late seventeen-hundreds, lay shrouded under almost three centuries of dense woodlands, mangled oak, pine and brambles along the far northeast outskirts of Angel Falls.

Josiah Krill joined the settlement town of Grangeville in 1698, several years before its name changed to Angel Falls. Rumors about Krill chronicled his apparent contempt for society. His dark persona was second only to his considerable wealth. An only child himself, Krill married but never had any children. He demanded the kind of privacy only a recluse would desire. One wonders what relief his old neighbors felt when he left Danvers, Massachusetts.

To maintain his privacy, Krill shipped in great stones hewn from a quarry in Pennsylvania. These stones were built into a ten-foot-high wall surrounding the twenty-acre wooded estate. He installed a heavy wrought-iron gate at the main entrance to the estate with "Ravenwood" emblazoned in an arc fifteen feet overhead. The remaining stones were built into his twenty-room, three-story mansion. The surrounding woods, in

Krill's time, held no shortage of ravens, their croaking calls echoing somberly in the shadows, hence the estate's name.

Krill, at seventy years of age, had some difficulty getting around. Because of this, and more importantly to maintain his privacy, he sent his servants, of which he had several, into town regularly for supplies. It was the absence of his personal presence in town that drove the rumor mill. His servants spoke little. Their uneasy demeanor suggested an employer who was, at best, difficult to serve or, at his worst, sadistic—if rumors are to be believed. Krill was, to say the least, an odd man shrouded in mystery.

More mysterious was the sudden departure of the servants. Early in 1722, Krill's servants became conspicuous by their absence. It had been several weeks since anyone remembered seeing them in town to buy supplies. Authorities dispatched to the mansion to check on the status of its residents returned with an astonishing report: Ravenwood had been deserted! There was no indication Josiah Krill, his servants, or anyone had ever occupied the estate!

Equally bizarre, all of the ravens had also vanished.

****

Having hitched a ride on route 51 north, sixteen-year-old Alex Sanders picked a random spot on the highway to be let off. From there he crossed the highway and began the trek west through grassy fields. He grabbed a bottled water from the side pocket of the gray backpack he had flung over his shoulder. Taking a couple sips of water, he then returned the bottle to the side pocket. After twenty-five minutes he turned northward and entered a heavily wooded area.

Old, unstable buildings get condemned. Sometimes these buildings simply disappear, remaining lost and forgotten. They stand as a monument to time, whether kind or unkind, way beyond their usefulness. Such is what Alex was about to stumble upon. A half hour into the woods, Alex found himself standing before a large, rusted wrought-iron gate barely visible beneath the heavy vegetation that clung to it.

The day, a Monday, was overcast and cool— perfect November weather to forget about textbooks and algebraic equations. A great time just to be alone with your thoughts. Alex could readily obtain the day's assignments from his friends at a later time. Unable to force the rusted gate open, Alex decided to follow the stone wall to see where it would lead.

It was slow-going as he worked his way eastward through tall weeds, vines, dead brambles and thorn bushes. The wall sometimes vanished completely beneath the heavy growth. When it did Alex would feel his way along. The vegetation was so dense in one area he almost missed a turn. He found the wall again where it turned to head north, along the eastern side of the estate. Moments later, he came upon an enormous, fallen oak tree. Its roots, completely torn from the earth. The enormous, fallen tree demolished a large portion of the wall where it had landed. The scene looked recent, within the last week or two, suggesting to Alex last Friday's severe rain and windstorm was the cause.

The breach in the wall allowed for easier access into whatever lay beyond. Through a small break in the forest canopy a jetliner far overhead left a thin vapor trail across the sky as it silently sailed beneath the clouds. It was the only indication of modern civilization Alex had seen since leaving Route 51. He climbed over the breach and inside the wall to continue west. The area was also thickly overgrown—more trees crowded his view and stood in his way.

Later, up ahead, Alex thought he could see a building hidden among the trees. Picking up the pace as best he could with low-growing vines grabbing at his ankles, an old house soon appeared. Fueled by curiosity he excitedly tripped up the stone stairs to a massive porch where he was confronted by a solid oak door, locked and immovable. The door's solid brass door knocker caught his attention so he raised the heavy object and let it drop. The resounding boom that followed echoed throughout the abandoned building sending a chill down his spine. It was then Alex realized how otherwise quiet his surroundings were. No wind rustled in the leaves and no birds sang. Not even a cricket could be heard. Looking around, Alex noticed a broken window at ground level to his right.

He jumped off the porch, reached the window, clambered up, and went inside the house. Once there, he was met by a heavier, darkness. A grave, oppressive spirit hung in the air. He pulled a flashlight from his backpack and pressed the switch but the light only flickered weakly. He shook the flashlight. It flickered on and off.

For a moment he thought something moved in the shadows. He shook the flashlight again. Something shadowy on the ceiling moved. The shadow suddenly swooped down directly towards him. He panicked, throwing himself to the floor, as he felt something leathery brush against his face. It flew past him and out the broken window.

A bat! Shaken, he continued to fiddle with the flashlight. He noticed the loosened battery enclosure. He twisted it tighter, breathing a sigh of relief as the light came on and stayed on. The steady light revealed old fashioned furnishings throughout the first floor. Tables, chairs, gas lamps, and a tall, silent grandfather clock occupied the room. Paintings hung on the walls, some hung lopsidedly, most covered with vines and moss, each displaying a scene from a time long gone. Tattered, grayed sheets covered some of the furniture. As Alex scanned the room with his light ghost-like shadows darted in and out of the light, like apparitions moving behind the furniture.

Only the occasional echo of water dripping from the ceiling or the buzz of an insect flying past Alex's head broke the otherwise immense silence. Alex kept alert to avoid stepping into a puddle or getting a face full of cobwebs. He let out a shriek when something small scurried between his feet.

The dining room contained the remains of someone's dinner, apparently interrupted in haste a very long time ago. The table, set with eight place settings of expensive-looking china and silverware, contained food remnants—the old bones of a cooked goose—and a basket once filled with bread. A few crumbs of bread remained, now rock-hard and moldy—embedded with evidence of some animal's teeth. Several serving bowls containing now unrecognizable items spread out across the table. Eight chairs surrounded the dining table; a few of them knocked over backwards.

Alex cautiously explored the rest of the first floor. Other rooms, also furnished, looked as if they had been untouched since forever ago. Spiders and cobwebs hung from every dark corner. Invading plant life and a damp chill in the air dispelled any sense of the mansion's former homeyness. Something wispy tickled the back of his neck. With a shiver Alex brushed away a spider dangling from the ceiling over his head.

Stepping further into the darkness, his grip growing tighter on the flashlight, Alex found a stairway to the second floor. It had a solid oak banister covered in vines. He cautiously made his way up the stairs when his heart suddenly stopped. Human eyes glared angrily down at him from the landing above. The face of an old man frozen in a twisted scowl warned all comers to approach no further.

Alex expelled a shuddering breath when he recognized it was just another oil painting. Perhaps a portrait of the original owner of the house. Taking a deep breath, he continued his ascent up the stairway somewhat unnerved by the loud creaks and groans each step produced. A thin layer of moss covered the stairs making them slippery in some areas. Once he reached the landing at the top, Alex was presented with a choice: turn left or right. He decided to turn down the hallway to his right.

He was about to inspect the first of several rooms opening onto the hallway but paused. A light 'knock-knocking' from the far end of the hallway caught his attention. Aiming his light in the direction of the noise he saw a door slowly swinging back and forth against the doorjamb. These other rooms could wait. Forgoing their exploration, Alex moved immediately to examine where this swinging door led.

A warped doorjamb prevented the door from closing completely. Alex put his hand out to stop the door's movement. When he released his hand the door started moving again. There were no drafts at the end of the hall, yet the door slowly continued to open and close on its own. He quickly dismissed, with a shudder, the notion some haunting spirit lingered in the old house. Alex pulled the door open. There he found another stairway ascending into utter darkness.

Attics. Filled with mystery or the allure of treasures hoarded by an eccentric from a long-forgotten age. Excited by the prospect of finding loot, Alex ascended the narrow passageway to the top. Reaching his destination, he found himself staring into a black void of dark shadows upon even darker shadows, until a faint glimmer of blue light shimmered from deep within the void. Alex turned to move toward it.

It was the last thing he ever did.

Chapter 3

Beverly Heartstone earned a new corner office at the Tribune, roomier and brighter than the old one. Two windows, one facing east, the other north, filled the room with more light and a greater view of downtown Angel Falls. Her new desk did not need old newspapers stuffed under one leg to keep it from wobbling. When Justin entered her office she greeted him with a wide smile and motioned for him to come in.

Justin took a cushiony chair opposite Beverly's as she took her plush seat behind her large maple-wood desk. She propped her feet up onto the corner of her desk, brushing back her shoulder-length brown hair. Justin handed her an envelope containing his bird pictures. She looked them over, humming as she did.

"You must be looking at the hummingbird picture," Justin said.

"Bad joke." Beverly moved past the hummingbird picture on to the next. The beautiful close-ups impressed her.

"I used a four-hundred millimeter, telephoto lens," He explained, anticipating her question.

"Even so, wouldn't you need to get close to get pictures like these?" she asked. "How is it they didn't fly away?"

"First, I tried my mind trick on the birds."

Beverly laughed. Justin continued, "I couldn't tell if it worked or not, but I still got the pictures!" he said.

"Patty gave me her article," she told Justin still sifting through the photos. These will go along nicely. We'll have a special full-color insert in recognition of Angel Falls' Three-Hundred-Twenty-Fifth Anniversary!"

"Going back to when it was Grangeville?" Justin asked.

"Yes-sir-ree! Grangeville, Angel Falls and all the crazy stuff since then!" she said.

Justin gave her a sideways glance. "You OK?"

"Never better—hey look, you have two crow pictures!"

Justin pointed to the picture in her left hand. "No, that one's a raven," he corrected.

Beverly looked closely at the photo. "There hasn't been a raven around here—in like forever! Where did you find this one?"

"I found dozens of them out past the Rogers' farm," Justin said.

"Way up there? You must have put some miles on the old Honda! I'm surprised it still runs!"

Justin smiled. His beat up Honda was often fodder for jokes. "It still gets me where I want to go."

Beverly, still impressed, looked over the photos again, humming as she did. This uncharacteristic behavior—light-hearted humming, putting her feet up on the desk—got the better of Justin's curiosity. It was nice to see her this way, but it was different from her usual all-business demeanor.

Watching her brought him back to three months ago when they both nearly died at the hands of the maniac, Siffer. His incredible Nephilim powers had been pitted against Justin's. In addition, Siffer enhanced his power by creating his own brand of nanobots. After stealing a sample of the bots from GenEx labs, he reverse engineered them. The he weaponized them for destruction and mind control. Ironically, these nanobots ultimately destroyed their creator.

Then there was the suicide. Beverly had watched as Dawn Stoltzfus stepped over the edge of the falls. Justin figured out the truth of Dawn's suicide and wondered if Beverly knew.

"Hey Bev…." he began cautiously, hoping not to upset her mood.

"Yes, Mr. Thyme?" She'd never called him "Mr." Thyme before.

"You remember Dawn. Did you know she was Siffer's niece?"

Beverly removed her feet from her desk, plopped them back onto the floor, and leaned forward, arms coming to rest on top of her desk. The smile on her face faded ever so slightly. "Sure. When I spied on Siffer's campaign headquarters it became apparent," She said.

"Did you know she has the Nephilim gene—the same as me and Siffer?" he asked her. "That's why I always had trouble reading her; she could block me."

Now her facial expression turned perplexed. "How many of you were there?"

How many of *you*. He was one of *them*. For an instant Justin felt the painful force of her choice of words. Her words would have hurt more, but his relationship to Beverly had grown more solid over several months of working together. He knew where she was coming from. Plus, she'd been exposed to supernatural horrors—difficult enough, more so because it wasn't part of her everyday belief system.

Justin explained. "Siffer's gone—for good. There's no need to worry about him. Dawn's harmless now. But she used her powers to make you think she went over the falls."

"The way you once fooled me into seeing two of you. So, she's still alive?"

"Apparently. But she left town for good—I believe her remorse was real. She'll never bother us again," Justin reassured her.

Beverly shifted her weight in her chair, crossed her legs and put her hand to her chin in deep thought. "I remember now! Her car was no longer at the scene. So, she drove it away herself!" she mused out loud. "Man, she really put me through the wringer!" After taking a moment to let those events sink in, her smile slowly returned.

Justin wanted to change the subject, but Beverly beat him to it. She mentioned the statue and the sword Justin used when battling Siffer. After the incident at Visitation Lake, the Park Service moved the statue to the Angel Falls Museum. They managed to force the sword back into its original position in the statue. A park ranger was able, using a mechanical device, to plunge it back through the chair and penetrate the stone base. To see what might happen, the ranger pulled back up on the sword. As if some mystical power held it there, it wouldn't budge!

"I'll have to bring you to the museum. We'll see if the legend still holds true: only someone with the Nephilim gene can remove it!" Beverly said with a smile.

"Don't expect a replay of the event—it was all I could do to prevent Siffer from ending your life!" Justin said.

"You dove right over me—right at the cliff's edge!"

"Don't remind me."

"Did you overcome your fear of heights after that?" Beverly asked.

Justin shuddered. "Not so much, really."

Justin and Beverly spent an unusual few minutes in quiet thought. Staring at the walls they recalled those awful days. Justin got uncomfortable and fidgeted. To relax, he took note of the paint on the walls of Bev's office. A very pale blue gave this office a cleaner look from her old one. Baseboards and doorframe were a slightly darker shade from the walls. His examination of the floorboards abruptly discontinued with a sudden outburst of nervous giggling. Something struck Beverly's funny bone.

"What on earth got into you?" Justin asked.

"I just had an awful thought!" Beverly explained trying to stifle further giggles. "One of your photos suddenly reminded me of a Lit course I had in college!"

"What are you talking about, which picture?"

"The raven."

"I thought you liked the picture. How is it awful?"

"Not the photo," she replied. "It's the ravens—they're a symbol of death or impending doom! Remember Edgar Allen Poe?"

"And that's funny?" Justin asked.

"Hey, some people laugh at funerals, I laugh at an imminent disaster!"

Her statement took him by surprise. "What disaster—what are you talking about?"

Beverly looked intently at Justin. "Think of it. No ravens for years. Now, suddenly, they show up. This is Angel Falls, Justin. First, angels save the town. Then a demonic lunatic tries to destroy it. Now the ravens are back—what else could it mean but trouble's headed our way?"

"Where's this coming from?" Justin asked. "You're making a bit of a leap from ravens to the Apocalypse, aren't you?

"Well, another thing: did you hear the weather report? The winds have shifted! What about that?"

Justin did not have an answer for her, but her questions left him with an uneasy feeling.

"I'm telling you," she said, "I feel we need to be careful!"

****

Tuesday brought another overcast November afternoon. Its chilling wind reminding everyone winter was not far away. An equally chilling death occurred this day. A body—along with associated evidence—might keep preserved in these colder temperatures, were it not for ravens now feeding upon it. But the cold also makes establishing a time of death more difficult.

Even without the feeding ravens, the body's gruesome appearance would make an identification of this unfortunate individual extremely difficult. The body, dried, withered and twisted—as if all life had literally been drained from it—no longer looked human. Because voracious ravens fully decimated what used to be the face, dental records would be required.

Resting in the tall grass where it lay, there appeared no indication the body had been dragged to its resting location. Only the grass beneath the body lay flattened, as if the corpse had fallen from the sky. As the swarm of noisy birds wrestled for sustenance, they very abruptly became silent. Then, as one, they looked skyward and swiftly flew off to the north.

One of New Horizons' part-time nurses ushered Jeb Wechsler into an empty examination room. "What brings you to the infirmary today, Mr. Wechsler?" she asked. Agnes Merrill practiced nursing part-time for the residents for the last fifteen years. She was slender, in her sixties, hair not quite reaching her shoulders.

"Headache!" was Wechsler's terse reply.

Nurse Merrill's calm and easy-going demeanor made her the perfect complement for the grumpy patient standing before her. "Have you tried aspirin?" she asked.

"Of course I have; it don't help!" was his answer. "It's been constant pain—for six days!"

"OK, Mr. Wechsler. You have a seat over there and I will have Doctor Craven come check you over," the nurse instructed him.

With a "Humph!" Wechsler sat down and waited, fidgeting with his fingers and looking anxiously around the room. It took another ten minutes before Doctor Craven arrived. By then, Wechsler was muttering angrily under his breath.

Doctor Brent Craven arrived at New Horizons a month earlier. About forty years old and trim, he wore the usual long white lab coat with a stethoscope hung around his neck. Dark, deep-set, squinting eyes, and short, jet black hair made him appear younger than his age.

The lack of a wedding ring indicated his single status, although he did sport a somewhat ornate ring on his right ring finger. Purportedly a family heirloom, the ring lacked luster and would have been better off hiding in a safe than adorning someone's finger.

Craven rarely smiled. His speech tended to be terse—straight to the point. Most of his New Horizons patients found him professional to a fault, although somewhat lacking in bedside manner.

Wechsler, however, just did not like the man.

"Good morning, sir! How is everything?" Craven said.

"How do ya think? I wouldn't be here if I was OK."

"I hear you have a nagging headache. On a scale of one to ten, ten being the worst pain, how would you rate your headaches?" Craven asked.

"Twenty!" Wechsler blurted.

Craven took an otoscope to look into Wechsler's nose and ears. Then he grabbed an ophthalmoscope to look into his eyes. Lastly, he checked Wechsler's blood pressure. It was a bit higher than usual, but Wechsler's current mood and pain might account for the increase.

"Have you been keeping up with your blood pressure meds?"

"That's what's makin' me sick!" Wechsler protested.

"I can make an adjustment to the dose, Mr. Wechsler, but you need to stay on your medication!" Craven cautioned.

"I felt better before I started takin' this stuff!" Wechsler barked.

Doctor Craven wrote out an adjusted blood pressure medication prescription and handed it to Wechsler. "See if it doesn't help with the headaches. Let me know."

"Oh, I'll let you know all right!" Wechsler said in a huff and dismissed himself.

****

Detective Tom Selden experienced a fairly slow week until a missing persons call came in. A student, Alex Sanders, who missed school two days ago, was still unaccounted for.

Selden, a slim twenty-seven-year-old, stood at six-foot-two with short, dark brown hair, sporting the usual blue suit with a solid-colored red tie and white shirt. He turned the case of the missing boy over to detective, Jake Henrycks, a returning native of Angel Falls. Henrycks arrived on the force five weeks earlier. His resume listed a tour of Afghanistan and work with Habitat for Humanity, among his accomplishments before he decided to join the police academy. Now at forty-one, the stocky, head shaved, five-foot-ten Henrycks had just transferred from the Philadelphia police force to return to his hometown to fight crime.

"He's about sixteen, last seen wearing a dark blue windbreaker and gray backpack," Selden passed the information along to Henrycks.

"Any ideas on his last location?" Henrycks asked.

"No, but he liked to hike wooded areas. You might start with those areas nearest his school and work to outlying areas from there," Selden said.

"What about friends?"

"Charles Underwood," Selden suggested. "I think they're in the same grade. Maybe he knew Alex and can shed some light on his habits."

Henrycks, after writing all this down on a notepad, pocketed it and headed out. Tom reached for his phone and dialed his friend at the Falls Tribune.

"Beverly here," came the lilting, cordial voice at the other end.

"Hi Bev, it's Tom. How's everything?"

"It's funny you should call! I had the oddest conversation with Justin the other day! What's on your mind?"

"What do you mean?" Tom asked. "And how is Justin?"

"He's OK. I told him we're in for another Angel Falls fiasco—complete with bad omens! Crazy huh?"

"You've become a bit more dramatic than usual, ever since—you know, Siffer and all," Selden said.

"Yeah, well…. Why *did* you call?"

"Actually, something *is* up, but not on your catastrophic scale. We've got a missing student," Selden said. "A young boy. But let's keep it out of the papers until we know more."

"Of course! How awful. How long has he been missing?"

"Couple of days. I have Jake on it," Selden said. "The kid never made it to school on Monday."

"Tom, something's up—I mean, half seriously, this feels like a precursor to another Angel Falls crisis."

"Based on what—your reporter's intuition?" Tom asked.

"Maybe. Maybe I'm still jittery over recent events," Beverly admitted.

"Or Justin is putting strange ideas in your head?" Tom taunted her.

"Just the opposite, Tom! He's been the down-to-earth one this time around!"

"Then go with that and stop worrying. I'll keep in touch—let you know anything new."

Chapter 4

Justin, Derrick, and CPU decided to meet at Justin's place. They hadn't been together much since CPU started back to school in late August. Derrick kept busy at his dad's auto body shop, Justin busied himself with his photojournalism job at the Tribune. CPU spent afternoons doing homework. Today they found some time off to sit lazily around the Thyme's living room and ruminate.

"A detective came to my house today," CPU said. "Asking a bunch of questions!"

"Who, Tom Selden?" Justin asked.

"No. An older guy," CPU said.

"Henrycks." Justin said. "Jake Henrycks."

"What'd you do now, Chuck?" Derrick asked. "Steal more jellybeans from your science teacher's desk?"

CPU glared at Derrick. "He wanted to know about some kid in my class, Alex Sanders."

"What about him?" Justin asked.

"Nobody has seen him for three days!" CPU said. "He asked if there was anything I knew about him—anything to help them find him."

"Next time," Derrick interrupted, "steal me some jellybeans. I like the red cinnamon ones!"

Justin elbowed Derrick and asked CPU, "You know this guy at all?"

"Not really," CPU said. "I tried to tell him that but he kept staring me down like I was hiding something!"

"Creepy!" Derrick admitted.

"He really spooked me! I was so glad for it to be over!" CPU said.

Justin remembered Alex kept mostly to himself. But that was all he knew about the missing boy. Derrick thought him rather wimpy. But, having been the football team's captain, he felt that way about most high-schoolers. Alex's mom and dad seemed normal; they always showed up at school functions, drove the standard minivan, and had a dog. Alex had no siblings and Justin, himself adopted, thought Alex may also have been adopted. But they all agreed: not much was known about Alex Sanders, which made his disappearance more mysterious.

"Isn't he the one who goes on long hikes?" Justin asked anyone who might have a clue.

"Beats me," Derrick said.

CPU made a face. "In this cold weather—and for *three* days?"

Derrick looked at Justin and asked, "Is your 'angel sense' tingling?"

"Negative," Justin replied. "Nothing since...you know...."

"Maybe things have been too quiet," CPU added.

"Let's not jinx things, CPU," Justin said. "Quiet is nice!"

****

The case of the missing student suddenly became the most unusual case to be dropped into the laps of Detectives Selden and Henrycks. Two hikers reported what they thought was a body three miles from the high school. When Henrycks investigated, he hardly recognized what lay in the field before him. Once he determined he had human remains, he sent for the coroner. Hopefully, Leslie Graves, the county Medical Examiner, could make a positive ID. A strong sense of dread plagued Henrycks and Selden. They'd have to rely on the ME's findings but felt fairly certain this horrific mangled carcass was once Alex. Busy at his desk, Tom Selden happened to look up just as Henrycks exited the elevator. Making straight for Tom's office, Henrycks quickly entered and dropped himself down onto a vacant corner of Tom's desk.

"He was in the middle of nowhere," Henrycks began, skipping any customary greetings. "Looks like no one else had been through there except for the hikers."

"Any signs of a struggle?" Tom asked

"Nothing!" Henrycks replied. "The entire area was devoid of evidence of any kind!"

Henrycks pulled an envelope from his suit's breast pocket. From the envelope he lifted several four-by-six glossies. He showed Tom the snapshots he took of the scene before the coroner arrived. Even a hardened detective like Tom cringed at the ghastly photos.

"On my way in I stopped at home first to print these," Henrycks said. "Took 'em with my cell."

"We'd better board these, even though I can't stand looking at them!" Tom said.

The detectives used a ten-foot by four-foot board to organize people, places, and anything else pertinent to an on-going case. Keeping all the facts in front of them during an investigation assisted in solving the case. It became obvious this case would require all the help they could get.

"That could be the remains of the windbreaker the boy was wearing," Tom said as he taped one of the photos onto the board. "But you're right, no real evidence here—he's not even wearing shoes!"

"We canvassed the entire area and found no sign of 'em," Henrycks said.

Tom asked, "Has the ME made any determinations yet—cause of death, anything? We need to tell the parents once she confirms the ID."

"Far from it. And how she'll determine *cause* of death is a mystery. But, I'll be in touch with the family once Graves gives me the word," Henrycks said.

"Did you talk to the ME in person?" Tom asked.

"Yeah. A real piece of work, ain't she?" Henrycks chuckled.

"Unusual sense of humor, maybe," Tom replied. "But she gets the job done!"

Tom dropped the remaining photos onto his desk and rubbed his face with both hands. He looked at Henrycks. "It's bad enough to bring news of a loved one's death. But when they look like this?"

"My own mother couldn't identify me, lookin' like that!" Henrycks said.

****

Jeb Wechsler managed to get himself to the New Horizons infirmary again. His headaches persisted, although not quite as severe. This time, however, he was experiencing a new ailment demanding Doctor Craven's attention.

"My hands shake!" Wechsler complained. "And I can't sleep!"

Craven performed a quick examination of Wechsler and came up with nothing unusual. His heart displayed a slight tachycardia, blood pressure was, again, up slightly. Wechsler's personality did not help his situation—always angry. His shaking hands could be the result of his cranky temperament or the lack of sleep. A lifetime of complaining will do harm to the nerves.

"There is a slight tremor, not terribly noticeable," Craven said. "It could just be a symptom of your age, nothing more."

"Well, *I* notice it! I ain't never had so many problems 'til you started me on them blood pressure pills!"

"Are the tremors worse during any particular time of the day?" Craven asked him. "Are there times when your hands are not shaking?"

"Worse at night—always shaking," Wechsler said. "And I'm more tired, but don't sleep!"

Doctor Craven considered the situation and made a recommendation. "Why don't I give you something to calm you down. It will also help you sleep at night. Perhaps all you need is better rest."

"More pills?" Wechsler grumbled.

Trying to calm his patient Craven said, "It will only be temporary—to see if it helps stop the shaking."

Wechsler grudgingly complied with the doctor's wishes and took the free samples Craven provided. The samples would last fourteen days. When the two weeks ended, Craven requested Wechsler return to be reexamined.

"Mr. Wechsler, I have to be somewhere else now," Craven said. "You be back here in two weeks, like I said, and we'll see if things have improved."

Wechsler left in a huff as Doctor Craven hurriedly removed his white lab coat, turned out the exam room lights, and left the infirmary. Twenty minutes later, he pulled his car up to the Medical Examiner's office and parked. Once inside he asked to speak to Leslie Graves and was directed to an examination room down the hall. He approached, knocked on the door and a woman in her fifties appeared.

"Yes, may I help you?" said Graves, glancing at her watch.

"I am Doctor Brent Craven from New Horizons."

"I am Doctor Leslie Graves from the Coroner's Office," she shot back. "It's getting late. What do you need?"

"Are you working on a severely distorted body found yesterday?" Craven asked.

Graves squinted and asked, "Why are you asking?"

"The body was found not far from New Horizons," Craven said. He tried to look past Graves' shoulder to get a peek at the corpse laid out on the exam table. "Sometimes an older resident might go missing. We had a minor incident at the facility recently. I was sent to look into it."

"Those old folks prone to running away?" Leslie asked.

"Not usually," Craven answered. "It's probably nothing—Sometimes relatives fail to check out a resident before taking them home for the weekend."

"Rest easy," Graves answered. "I can tell you is this was not a senior citizen, but a young man."

"What a relief!" Craven said. "I mean for New Horizons—but what a tragedy! How young was the boy?"

"Yes, a relief...don't like getting sued, eh?" Graves said with a laugh. "About sixteen—school age. And I hate to cut this short but I've still more work to do here."

"Who was he?" Craven asked

"That information won't be released until next of kin gets notified. Is there anything else?"

"How'd he die?" Craven asked.

"Like I said, more work to do," Graves said.

"Thanks for the help, Doctor." Craven began to leave, but stopped short and asked, "When do you expect to release the body?"

Graves hesitated before answering. This guy had an awful lot of questions. "I suspect it'll take me another few days before I can make a final determination on this case. Afterwards, he goes back to his family for cremation."

"You've been much help, Miss Graves. Thanks!" Craven said as he turned and headed back the way he came.

"Sure thing, doc," Graves called back. "And it's Mrs.!"

Leslie Graves went back to the body. She looked down at the withered mass on the cold, steel table. "You poor thing! Tomorrow we'll see if we can't figure out what happened to you."

The hour was late. Graves called to her assistant, Rachel, to lock up the exam room after she left; she was tired and wanted so much to get home. Maybe a good night's sleep would bring back the old pizazz. At this moment, however, she had no idea what steps she would take to figure out how Alex ended up the way he did. Upon leaving, Graves turned to the body, "Don't wait up for me!"

When her assistant, Rachel, got around to checking Graves' exam room the lights were already off. She tried the door—locked. Everything inside looked as it should, body and all. Rachel figured her boss, stressed by this case as she was, absent-mindedly locked up after all. Locking her lab was second nature to her, something she probably did without thinking about it.

****

A lightly drifting snowfall the next morning laid a somber pall over Angel Falls. Friday's obituaries opened with one particularly sad story. Among the elderly individuals more often found on these pages, one Alex Sanders appeared. A mere sixteen years old, Alex would not make it to his seventeenth birthday. Mercifully omitted were the gruesome details about the condition of the deceased. A short paragraph only mentioned Alex attended Falls High and had been on the track team. Survived by his parents, the closed-casket funeral would be held on Monday.

Justin, not generally prone to peruse the obituaries, happened to see this one. The current photo of the once living Alex triggered something in him. A vague, momentary impression overcame him. It did not strike him as forcefully as the first vision he had on his eighteenth birthday. But like Spiderman's 'spidey-sense,' he suddenly knew there was more to Alex's death—something. A sudden chill tickled his spine.

It was enough to make him pick up his home's land line and call Beverly. When she answered, she sounded less cheery than the last time they spoke.

"I had a feeling you might call," she said.

"I had a feeling too—an angelic sensation, one about the dead student, Alex," Justin said.

"I saw the crime scene photos, Justin. Unfortunately, this one looks right up your alley!"

"Why do you say that?" Justin asked.

"They had to go with dental records to determine who the victim was," she said.

Beverly explained the unearthly condition of the body. There were no signs of a struggle. Leslie Graves filled her in on some of the details of the scene, the specifics of which Beverly deliberately left out of the newspaper. No needle marks were found on the body, no discernible drugs in what little was left of the internal organs. There were no burns or chemicals present, yet the skin was twisted, shriveled, and leathery. The bones, when pressed hard enough between the fingers, splintered or turned to dust! Graves confirmed: nothing like this had ever presented itself in the history of the coroner's office!

Beverly continued, "The ME found only one small piece of evidence—what she thinks is a human hair. She's waiting for DNA confirmation with the hope it might ID the killer."

"So you think it's happening again?" Justin asked.

"I was in a mood the other day, not *totally* serious, but now...."

"Now that I've had one of my quirky visions," Justin cut in.

There was a time, when Beverly first met Justin, she considered his help more of an interference. Police matters were not meant for civilians. All this occurred before she knew what he was capable of and before she learned to trust in him as a friend. Even so, it came as a bit of a shock to Justin when she asked him to get involved in the matter!

If the demise of Alex turned out to involve something—she hated the word, *supernatural*—Justin *should* be involved. Tom Selden was an excellent detective, but Justin added the extra edge she knew they'd need to solve this kind of case. After an extended amount of pleading with him, Justin reluctantly agreed. He knew he'd have to avail himself of Derrick's and CPU's valuable help. Their loyalty was unquestionable, yet he wondered. With the battle against Siffer so recent in their minds, would his friends be ready to get involved with something this grotesque?

****

Ryan Bosley and his girlfriend Gwen Phillips strolled the wooded path along the north shore of Falls River. A full moon intermittently emerged between tree branches above, lighting the path and their faces as they walked arm in arm. Wrapped inside heavy coats and gloves to provide protection against the cold, crisp night air, the couple spoke in hushed tones between moments of suppressed laughter. Beyond the trees to their right the low rumble of the river's flow had a tranquilizing effect on the couple. Most of the evidence of the light snow from earlier in the day had vanished.

They spoke of school, life at home, and friends—avoiding any conversation about their feelings for each other. Both were a little nervous about being alone together for the first time. As darkness closed in around them, they huddled closer together.

One name came up as they spoke. It was the name of their mutual friend, Jim Fallow. Expecting to see him earlier that afternoon, Jim failed to show. That morning Ryan received a text from Jim explaining his intention to meet them after taking care of a personal matter. The plan was to double date—a matinee double-feature started at one o'clock in the afternoon. Apparently Jim never called his girlfriend to confirm the time as she also failed to show up.

Ryan and Gwen ended up seeing the movies without their friends. However, the day turned out better than expected. Being alone, it allowed them to get to know each other better. They grabbed something to eat after the final movie let out and then went for a walk.

Up a little further, the path they followed disappeared into heavy vines and low-growing bushes. They turned aside to find a way around the overgrown area when something on the ground ahead caught Gwen's eye. Then Ryan saw it as well, shining in the moonlight.

Suddenly, Gwen let out a scream. Ryan's blood froze in his veins. Empty eye sockets stared back at them from something resembling a human face, its twisted, gaping jaw appeared to scream in agony. What appeared to have been a human body, lay contorted, leathery and pale, in a heap on the ground in front of them.

Gwen regained enough composure to find her cell phone to dial 911. Ryan cautiously approached the body. It still gripped something in its right hand. He gingerly worked the object from the corpse's stiff hand. It was a cell phone—Jim's phone! Knowing Jim's passcode, Ryan open it. He checked Jim's messages and looked for recent calls.

Gwen looked at Ryan, wide-eyed and trembling.

Ryan held up the phone. "It's Jim's phone," he whispered.

Gwen pointed at the mangled body on the ground. "You think *this* is Jim?"

Ryan paged through the emails and messages. Suddenly, something awful jolted him. "Gwen, look at this!"

She reached for the phone. "It's a text—so?"

Ryan's voice became anxious. "See who it's from?"

"Yeah, Alex," Gwen said.

"Right! Alex—sent this morning! He's asking Jim to meet him behind the high school today! Gwen, Alex has been dead several days! There's no way he sent this text today!"

"Put the phone back, Ryan!" Gwen urged. "It might be contaminated!"

Ryan shuddered. He placed the phone back into the corpse's hand as the wail of sirens suddenly pierced the night in the distance.

"Let's go—the cops are coming," Gwen said. "Let them take care of this!"

"They'll want us to give a statement," Ryan said.

Gwen looked intently at Ryan. "We could end up like Jim. Let's get away from here!"

Ryan looked around for the best escape route to avoid the approaching cops. Making sure no one saw them, he grabbed Gwen's hand. Together they slipped and stumbled up the grassy embankment then hotfooted it down the road. Out of breath they stopped a moment to steal a hasty glance toward the location of the body. Mere seconds later, the first of several patrol cars arrived at the scene.

Chapter 5

On Saturday, Justin, Derrick, and CPU sat around Derrick's living room to do some brainstorming. CPU had his laptop, Derrick brought along his overblown imagination. News of a second, identical murder hit the newsstands early in the morning. This time the story contained a few of the gory physical details the deceased had in common, but no pictures. It also mentioned Alex's missing backpack and the text message on Jim's cell phone. The hair found on Alex's body did not get reported.

Derrick bandied about several of his own theories with CPU.

"A giant snake ate him!" Derrick proposed. "Then pooped him out!"

CPU shot him a look of disgust. "No aliens from outer space this time?"

"I'm serious—an anaconda makes sense!" Derrick objected. "How else could they end up that way?"

"Anacondas do not actually eat people, Derrick," CPU corrected, "besides, there are no anacondas in Angel Falls!"

Justin laughed. "Maybe the space aliens are intelligent anacondas!"

"OK, acid then," Derrick proposed. "A mad scientist dipped them in acid!"

"According to the paper acid was not involved!" CPU said. "Anyway, where is the motive?"

"So give us your brainy idea, Chuck!" Derrick said. "You're the guy with the high IQ!"

"Alex usually carried his phone in his backpack," CPU said. "Find the phone, find the backpack! Maybe his phone will tell us where he spent his last moments!"

Justin was well acquainted with CPU's abilities with electronics. Knowing Alex's last known whereabouts could get them some answers. The authorities seemed to have little else to go on. He asked CPU to give his idea a try.

CPU opened his laptop and brought up the app 'Fone Finder'. Entering Alex's phone number, CPU fiddled around as he tried to guess Alex's password. Bingo! Suddenly a red dot appeared on the map. He gave out a "Whoop!" and clapped his hands. Derrick and Justin checked out the map on the screen. The dot appeared near the far northeast corner of Angel Falls.

"It's out in the middle of nowhere!" Derrick grumbled.

"Miles from where the body was found," Justin reminded them. "If we take Highway 51 and park here," indicating a spot off the road on the map, "we can walk the rest of the way."

With enough daylight to get the job done, the three packed their lunches, some water bottles, and three flashlights into one backpack. CPU closed the laptop and checked the charge on his cell phone. It had the same 'Fone Finder' app installed. He'd use the phone app to pinpoint the location of Alex's phone once they got closer to its location. Derrick disappeared for a few minutes. He returned wearing a pith helmet. A machete hung from his belt at his side.

"You look like something out of Jumanji," Justin said. "And a machete! You think it's necessary?"

"The area's all dense woods," Derrick said. "It could come in handy."

CPU muttered, "Something is sure dense, but not the woods—Hey!" Derrick swung the pith helmet across the back of CPU's head. "That hurt!"

Justin interrupted, "Let's go, you guys. Time's a-wastin'."

Once in the Honda, they headed east toward Highway 51, then took 51 north. They drove for about twenty-five minutes until they reached a spot where, on the other side of the road, they could pull over and park. CPU opened 'Fone Finder' on his cell. The red dot appeared a mile from their current position. From here they decided to walk the rest of the way. Justin and CPU made Derrick carry the backpack in order to, as they said, "complete his ensemble." The walk was fairly easy across the grassy pasture until things took on an ominous appearance. Miles of dense forest, dark and foreboding, now emerged directly in front of them.

CPU checked his phone app and pointed out the direction they should go. "Through those woods."

Justin swallowed hard. "This should be interesting."

CPU laughed nervously. "Go ahead, Jack Black. Lead the way!"

Derrick shifted the heavy backpack onto his shoulders. "Yeah, well keep up squirt!" he ordered.

After a while the woods became so dark, even during daylight, the use of their flashlights became necessary. Derrick correctly surmised these woods would be dense! When a half hour had passed Justin thought he could see something up ahead. He pointed it out to his friends.

Even with his flashlight, CPU could see nothing. "Where?"

"Just up ahead," Justin answered, still pointing straight ahead.

Then Derrick understood. "It's your angel-powered eyes. I forgot you see better in the dark than we do," he said.

"It's a wall, mostly overgrown by all the foliage," Justin said. "Straight, that way."

"That area is right in line with my red dot," CPU added.

It took another five minutes of walking before a tall iron gate bearing the name 'Ravenwood' stood in their way. It stood slightly ajar with a large, broken tree limb preventing them from simply pushing the gate open the rest of the way. The opening was too narrow to squeeze through, even for CPU. The wall and gate would be too difficult to climb. Justin knew what to do—a maneuver he performed once before.

He had CPU and Derrick stand back as he walked up very close to the gate. Closing his eyes, he concentrated on being on the other side of the gate. A moment later the leaves at his feet began to stir creating a mini-cyclone around him. The leaves rose into the air, encircling him ever faster. A bright light formed at Justin's shoulders then suddenly spread out, bursting with a blinding flash. Justin no longer stood outside the gate. He waved at his friends from inside the estate, wearing a wide grin.

Derrick, wide-eyed, stood outside looking in and exclaimed, "That never gets old!"

"Nice!" CPU added.

Justin looked around. His grin suddenly faded. He just expended incredible energy to get inside. His mind, in his weakened, susceptible state now became ultra-sensitive. The wind appeared to pick up. Overhead, boney, razor-sharp tree limbs reached down for him, clawing at him. A million ravens surrounded him. They cried out from the darkness their raspy calls piercing his ears and echoing inside his head.

Abruptly, the wind died. Justin regained his composure. His mind became calm and he remembered why he was there.

"Justin, you OK?" Derrick called.

"OK. Yes," Justin replied. "I just had the worst vision!"

"We must be getting close to something!" CPU said.

Glancing down at his feet, Justin saw a large tree limb wedged up against the gate. It prevented the gate from opening all the way. He tried to pull the limb away. Being immobilized by numerous, heavy vines it wouldn't budge. In his still weakened condition, he called to Derrick.

"Uh, Derrick?"

"Yes, Justin?"

"Can you pass me your machete through the gate, please?"

"Where's your super strength, man?" Derrick asked.

"I temporarily used it up to get in here! You know how it is!"

With a rather smug, dramatic flair, Derrick withdrew the machete from his side, waved it in the air a few times, then passed it to Justin. "I *knew* this would come in handy, *CPU*!" he said, giving his younger friend a sneer.

Justin grabbed the machete. For three minutes he hacked away at the vines. Finally, with the limb freed, he passed the machete back to Derrick. With angelic strength returned, Justin lifted and tossed the heavy tree limb to the side. Derrick pushed the gate open and he and CPU stepped inside the dark estate grounds.

"Where to now, boss?" Derrick asked CPU.

CPU looked at his phone and pointed. "Straight ahead, that way."

After another few minutes, Justin saw the outline of a building. Moments later, they were climbing a massive stone stairway up to a porch. They admired the aged, moss-covered stone architecture. A huge oak doorway embellished with a solid brass door knocker now stood in their way. Derrick lifted the massive knocker, tarnished with age, and let it drop. A resounding boom broke the dark silence as it echoed throughout the woods.

CPU jumped. "Who are you expecting to answer?"

Derrick gave CPU a *'what's it to you?'* look. "I like door knockers; I just wanted to try it,"

"It was loud enough to wake the dead!" Justin said.

It was at that moment Justin noticed a broken window off to their right. Transporting himself through the gate drained him enough physically he did not want to try it again with this heavy door. So the three of them took the easier route and climbed in through the window.

Their flashlights illuminated the interior sufficiently to evaluate their surroundings. It became immediately obvious this place had been vacant for a long, long time. Sheet-covered chairs and tables swayed and danced like ghosts with each pass of their flashlights. Cobwebs, insects, some bats, rats and a raccoon made up the remaining décor. Patched with areas of a fine moss, the musty dampness reached their nostrils. CPU sneezed loudly.

"Gesundheit!" Justin said.

"*Good Housekeeping* should do a story on this place," Derrick said carefully taking in his surroundings.

"Or *Better Homes and Gardens*!" CPU said.

Justin laughed. "*Ghoul Housekeeping* or *Better Horrors and Ghouls* would be more like it!"

They took some time to explore the first floor. If this was Alex's last stand they wanted to know what happened. And where was the backpack and phone—according to CPU's app it was very close.

"This looks like my grandmother's place," Derrick noticed.

"More like your grandmother's grandmother's grandmother," Justin said.

CPU saw something on the floor. At first he thought it was a button. A closer look revealed it to be an old coin.

"My dad collects rare coins," Derrick said. "Here's a real old one—maybe eighteenth century!"

CPU looked in awe at his rare find. "If this belonged to the original owner, then this house must be hundreds of years old!"

"Based on the upkeep of the place, you're probably right," Derrick observed.

Derrick was ready to tear the place apart to search for more rare coins, but Justin reminded him of the purpose of their trek out here. Sunlight was also becoming a rare commodity. It was agreed: find the backpack. Later, when they got home, they would look up 'Ravenwood' and find out more about the coin. They might even come back to look for more.

When the backpack failed to show up on the first floor, they found a stairway to the second floor and started the climb up. CPU went first, followed by Derrick, then Justin. One stair groaned, then another, breaking the near-dead silence. The antique, musty wallpaper pictured various horse and carriage scenes, men in top hats and women wearing hoop skirts carrying umbrellas. The hard wood stairs lacked a carpet covering and were cracked along the grain from water damage. A thin film of moss on a few steps made them dangerously slippery.

"Don't fall, Chuck!" Derrick called up the stairs. "You'd crack your head open on these stairs!"

"I would first fall into you, cushioning *my* fall and cracking open *your* head!" CPU retorted.

Justin chimed in, "Derrick, you *are* a difficult target to miss!"

Suddenly, CPU let out a horribly loud shriek. Derrick pointed his flashlight up toward CPU and froze. It was at the top of the stairs, the thing that had CPU transfixed with fright. Justin saw it too.

Once he regained his composure, Derrick found his voice. "It's...it's just a painting, CPU," he said.

"Those eyes..." CPU whispered.

"Yeah, Chuck. Gave me the skin crawlies too!"

Justin ran up the remaining steps, careful to watch his footing. He passed CPU to get a closer look at the life-sized portrait. An elderly man, pictured seated from his lap, up, glared straight down at him.

"The plaque at the bottom says, 'Josiah Krill,'" Justin said.

"Maybe *he* was the owner," Derrick said. "Hey, Chuck, you gonna be OK?"

"Sure, sure!" CPU said with a shiver. "Not very jolly, was he?"

"Maybe he wants his coin back," Justin scoffed.

Once all three reached the landing two directions became open to them: go left or go right. They decided to take the hallway to their right. The first doorway they came to opened with a light creak. Three flashlights came to rest upon what looked like a master bedroom. A large tree limb had broken through the ceiling. The bed was made. Sitting on the night table next to it was an oil lamp. A water pitcher and bowl sat on the sturdy oak dresser at the other end of the room, under a window.

A once expensive-looking oriental rug lay on the floor at the foot of the bed. Water-stained, some undefined odor wafted up from it. CPU sneezed again. Walls decorated with wallpaper contained similar olden-days themes as the wallpaper on the first floor. Mostly intact, but dotted with damp areas and some peeling, it bore evidence to the quality of work put into the construction of this mansion. Certainly, it had seen better days!

Three other rooms along the hallway, also bedrooms, had similar furnishings, but no backpack and no phone. Fone Finder indicated they were going in the right direction and getting closer. They continued to search the rooms down the hallway until, at the end of the hall, they reached one last door. It was locked. Justin shone his flashlight around the end of the dark hallway looking for something useful to pry the door open. His light came to rest on a tarnished metallic object on the floor. He recognized what turned out to be an old-style skeleton key.

He reached down for the key and handed it to Derrick. "Here. Try this."

With a bit of pressure, the key turned but the door would not open.

Derrick pulled on the doorknob. "It's stuck tight!"

CPU laughed. "Is that all you got, big guy?"

That kind of taunting got Derrick angry and he grabbed the doorknob harder. With a yell he gave a terrific yank. The door swung open violently almost hitting him in the face.

Derrick examined the door. "It's warped—no wonder it wouldn't open easily!"

Justin went to close the door and, sure enough, it would not close completely without a hefty shove, which he decided not to try. Behind the door another twenty steps emptied into black nothingness at the top. Their flashlights revealed only enough to see the wood beams of the ceiling from their vantage point.

"Looks like the attic," Derrick said. "Shall we?"

The stairs were steep and narrow; a few missing stairs made an occasional, quick jump necessary. After the careful climb they made it to the top and stepped inside. Their flashlights brightened only a small portion of large room at a time. Against the wall to their left stood a seven-foot tall by four-foot wide mirror framed in ornate oak carvings depicting birds and grapevines. To their right, four stacks of large dusty, stained boxes sat piled three or four high.

At the far end of the dingy room, their lights rested upon a small window darkened by a heavy layer of soot. On the windowsill a human skull held a large candle. Built into the bench below the window, bookshelves filled with leather-bound volumes ran the length of the entire wall. An antique refractor telescope in one corner of the room, sat atop a tripod.

The boys moved slowly about the room, glancing their lights here and there as they looked around. One large table, open books and astrological charts sprawled over its surface, took position in the center of the attic.

CPU noticed several pairs of lights peeking beyond the outer limits of his flashlight—blinking in the darkened corners of the attic. He took a step back; something brushed the top of his head. He looked up.

"Aayyyee! It's coming for me!" he howled as he dove for the floor.

Huge, outstretched talons plunged for his head, eyes glowing, eager for prey!

Derrick turned his flashlight in CPU's direction and let out a loud whistle. "Charles, take it easy!" he said. "It's stuffed—hanging by a wire!"

CPU sat up, wiped his forehead with his shirtsleeve. "Man! My heart's pounding—I'm sweating!"

"You're also using contractions!" Derrick noted. "I thought you gave up on them—too *crass* for your style!"

"Never mind!" CPU mumbled. "I lost it for a moment!"

Justin picked up a dusty volume from the table entitled, *The Necromancer*. "Whoever lived here dabbled in the occult," he said.

CPU, still shaken from what turned out to be a stuffed owl, said, "The only thing missing is a Ouija Board."

Next, they checked out the stacks of boxes. More books—mostly very old, along with rolled up parchments containing odd symbols. Derrick, convinced one of the parchments had dried blood on it, declined to handle any more of the rolled up papers. Inside one of the boxes was an enormous, three-foot diameter world globe. It caught CPU's interest because the continents looked nothing like their counterparts on a modern world globe. It sat loosely on a pedestal. He tried to get a better look but was unable to pull it out of the box.

"Derrick, can you put this on the table?"

Derrick strained to lift the globe from the box. "Good Night! What's this thing made of, lead?" he grunted.

"Just put it over on the table, please!" CPU said.

With a 'thud' the globe dropped onto the table. CPU looked it over, trying to spin it on its pedestal, but it barely moved due to its massive size. It appeared to be ceramic, which could account for its weight. Not very practical, he thought, especially if you can't make it turn on its axis. As he expected, names of countries were out of date. This globe had to be ancient, he surmised. No way it came from a Five and Ten store so it had to be worth something!

All these artifacts, rare books, and maps would have cost a fortune, even in Krill's time. Obviously, the stories of the man's wealth were not exaggerated! From his studies, CPU knew of the 'Earth Apple' globe, the oldest know globe in existence, dating back to 1492. Krill's globe somewhat resembled pictures he'd seen of the 'Earth Apple.' Fascination slowly replace the creepiness of the attic—then something else caught the corner of CPU's eye.

"Look! The backpack!" he shouted. From his viewpoint the backpack sat tucked in a corner behind the boxes.

"So, Alex was here!" Derrick said. "We are like some kind of detectives!"

Justin grabbed the backpack and set it down on the floor in front of the mirror. Inside they found Alex's Track and Field jersey, flashlight, a half-finished bottle of water, and his cell phone.

CPU grabbed the phone. "Only nine percent charge left."

"So what do we do with it now?" Derrick asked.

"We check his emails and messages when we get back," Justin said. "Maybe they'll tell us something."

Justin threw everything back into the backpack when he heard something. The attic stairs! "Someone's coming!" he whispered. "Hide!"

They three scurried to the darkest places behind the stacks of boxes as the sound of approaching footfalls grew louder.

Justin waved frantically at Derrick, pointing at his light. "Turn your flashlight off!" he mouthed.

Someone entered the room. At first, it was too dark to clearly see the face, but they could tell it was a man. The man immediately saw the backpack in front of the mirror. He went over to it. Giving the room the once over with his flashlight, the man picked up the backpack, made a quick about-face, and retreated back the way he came.

Keeping his voice low, CPU turned to Derrick who had hunched down next to him behind the boxes. "That was Detective Henrycks!" CPU said.

"How can you tell?" Derrick asked. "I couldn't see."

"His bald head—I saw it reflected in his flashlight! CPU said. "Plus, I will never forget those eyes!"

Justin joined them from his hiding place. "He's right. It was Henrycks."

"Did you see how he went straight for the backpack? It's like he already knew it would be here!" CPU said.

"Maybe he found it the same way we did," Justin said. "GPS tracking."

"Or, maybe he knows more than he's letting on!" CPU said. "And do not tell me I am overly suspicious!"

Justin shook his head. "CPU, he's the lead detective on the case; he's looking for clues, like we are."

"And he's long gone by now, let's get out of here," Derrick said.

The three started for the exit.

CPU stopped suddenly. "Yikes, what was that?" He did a one-eighty to aim his light at something behind the boxes where they had been hiding.

"Nobody says 'Yikes!'" Derrick quipped.

"What is it?" Justin asked. "There's nothing's back there."

"Something moved! I saw it reflected in the mirror!" CPU told him.

"Probably a raccoon," Derrick said.

"It was bigger than a raccoon, Derrick," CPU insisted.

Justin went back to the boxes and shined his light around for CPU's benefit. "I don't see anything—sorry!"

Derrick went to the door. "Let's go! It's getting darker outside, plus this place is starting to give me the Heebie Jeebies!"

They got to the door and headed down the attic stairs. As they descended, Derrick heard CPU mutter under his breath from behind, "Nobody says 'Heebie Jeebies!'"

Exiting the house the way they entered— through the window—the three cautiously made their way back to the gate.

"I don't see any sign of Henrycks," Justin whispered. "But stay alert!"

"Yeah, we don't want to get caught snoopin' around a possible crime scene!" Derrick added.

"Would this still be considered private property?" CPU asked.

"Another reason not to be caught here!" Derrick said.

"And I don't want to get lost in these woods when the sun goes down!" Justin added.

The sun was just beginning to set in the horizon the same time the boys successfully made it to Justin's car. There had been no sign of the detective anywhere. Because they lost the opportunity to examine Alex Sander's cell phone, they decided instead to drive directly to the library. There they'd see what they could learn about Ravenwood.

The Honda sputtered and purred as they got under way.

"We had the phone and lost it!" CPU grumbled.

"At least we know Sanders was there," Derrick said.

"Where does an old mansion fit into all this?" CPU asked.

"Based on the occult materials we found inside," Justin said, "and knowing this is Angel Falls, I'm betting there's something awful brewing!"

"Enough reason never to go back there!" Derrick said, remembering what happened to him after he drank Siffer's punch. "Let's move! I hear Florida's nice."

Chapter 6

Back in the sixties the Angel Falls library transferred extremely old newspapers and documents to microfiche before they could crumble into dust. Additionally, newspapers, magazines, maps, almost any kind of written material produced up until 1958 were on microfiche. Anything beyond 1958 to 1990 got cataloged, sorted, labeled, and organized in the large basement of Angel Falls library. These were open to the public for viewing. All information after 1990 got transferred onto computers.

It took Justin, Derrick, and CPU about an hour before they found any relevant information on microfiche about Ravenwood. The estate cost $40,000 in the 1790s, which is equivalent to almost $1,200,000 today. Although the owner, Josiah Krill, was indeed a wealthy individual, he was not a very happy camper. The sketch they found of Krill in one of the newspapers, looking as grumpy as the portrait inside the mansion, confirmed that.

Write-ups of Krill painted a picture of someone of suspicious behavior. This became particularly true owing to the sudden disappearance of his entire household. Article after article made it quite clear: something at Ravenwood Estate was amiss. Artists' renditions of Krill, his servants, and the mansion's interior also appeared in the old newspapers. It was decades before photography would be invented, but the detail of the sketches looked remarkably accurate and realistic based on the portrait they saw.

"His eyes are creepy, like Detective Henrycks'," CPU said looking at a sketch of Krill.

"His interrogation really rattled your cage, didn't it?" Derrick said. "Get used to the fact: that's the way detectives assigned to this case will act!"

Justin interrupted. "Why does Danvers, Massachusetts sound familiar?"

"What about it?" Derrick asked.

Justin pointed to a line in one of the papers. "See? It's where Krill's from originally."

CPU prided himself in his knowledge of Angel Falls history. "Most settlers came from New York, Pennsylvania, and Delaware. Not many arrived from New England."

Justin decided to let the question go for now. What really interested him was the bizarre nature of Krill's disappearance plus the equally bizarre condition of Alex Sanders. What happened to Krill and his entourage? What drew Alex to Krill's mansion—what was the connection, if there was one? Could Ravenwood Estate have been cursed by the mansion's occupants. In Justin's experience, multiple bizarre circumstances linked by a connection, however tenuous, was a sure sign of Angel Falls-sized trouble.

"This section lists some of Krill's employees' names," Derrick noted, pointing to the microfiche. "He had a cook, maids, a butler—even a farrier who took care of the horses."

"I don't remember seeing a stable," CPU said.

Derrick scanned ahead in the article. "Looks like it burned to the ground about the same time everyone vanished. It says a lightning strike caused the fire."

Justin, sitting at a second microfiche, discovered more about Krill. "He traveled the world—owned his own ship, 'The Elinor'. He hired people from different countries as he traveled. Says here they stayed with him; they all migrated to Grangeville together."

"The guy must've been rolling in money!" Derrick said. "His cook came from France, two Spanish maids, it even mentions a nurse from England."

"The ship is named after his wife," CPU added. "Grumpy actually had a wife!"

After another half-hour, a call over the library PA system announced the late time. Soon the library would be closing. The trio finished up, putting all the papers back where they belonged, but not before using their cell phones to take photos of information they found pertinent to the case. Should they need to investigate further it would save them from additional trips to the library. So far, however, what they discovered stirred up even more questions than they had before.

The boys sat in silence as they drove from the library to Justin's. Once there, CPU and Derrick walked home. At Henson Road they split up, each having about three blocks more to reach their respective homes. It was a little past sundown, but a nearly full moon offered some additional light to the streets below. CPU suddenly stopped short of his own house. Spotting something up ahead he dashed behind a car and crouched down to watch. Detective Henrycks was across the street, questioning a young man. Fellow classmate Brian Cosgrove was being interrogated in front of his own home.

He could not hear anything being said, but CPU saw Cosgrove shrug like he had no answer for whatever Henrycks just asked him. The questioning continued for another minute or two when Henrycks abruptly turned and headed for his car parked nearby. Cosgrove shook his head; he watched Henrycks drive off before going inside his home. CPU ran the rest of the way home, ran inside, shut the door, and locked it.

****

Justin knocked on Beverly's office door. She waved him in as he took his usual seat across from hers. She usually gave him new assignments over the phone. For some unknown reason she called for a face-to-face meeting, which had him a bit curious.

After some small talk, Beverly got to the point. She wanted an update of Justin's investigation into the killings. Her interest peaked upon hearing Justin tell of the old mansion in the woods. She remembered old stories she heard as a kid about a creepy, abandoned building in the woods. As far as she knew, no one ever mentioned actually going there. These were just stories, until now.

The stories included hauntings with eerie sounds coming from the woods at night—all the standard nonsense attributed to abandoned places. Knowing the dead boy's belongings wound up at this house certainly stirred her curiosity. Her reporter's training compelled her reporter's mind to remain on the Fact Wagon. Justin's news, however, pushed her into the realm of Fantasy.

She listened intently as Justin described the inside of the mansion, Krill's reclusiveness, his treatment of his servants.

"Some elaborate maps and rare books on the occult filled his attic," Justin said. "As well as birds of prey mounted everywhere."

"No skulls or shrunken heads?" Beverly smirked.

"Actually, one skull holding a candle!" Justin laughed. "A telescope too."

"He could have been an astrologer or astronomer," Beverly suggested.

"Get this, his entire household completely vanished one day without a trace."

Beverly leaned back in her chair. "That is bizarre! I'd have wondered about his sanity," she said, "It's better history has forgotten him."

"Some of the stuffed birds were ravens; plenty of live ones swarm the woods around his place now."

"Well, there you have it! The sudden disappearance of a reclusive astrologer, unearthly murders, creepy birds, a haunted mansion, the occult—it all fits together!"

Justin thought she was half joking. But her nervous laugh gave her away. He eyed her curiously. "*Murders?* You said 'murders', as in *more* than one?"

She then dropped a bombshell—the other reason she called him in.

"A *second* body!" Justin reeled in his chair. "Who?"

"Jim Fallow," Beverly said. "Without the dental records he would have been completely unidentifiable."

"Just like Alex Sanders?" Justin asked.

"Exactly," she replied.

Beverly told Justin the detectives had looked into a possible terrorist connection but dismissed the idea. The coroner found no trace evidence of chemicals on the bodies. No lye, lime, or acids that might account for the two boys' freakish, yet identical condition. There was no trace of explosive materials either. They were completely clean of any chemical contaminants.

"We may be looking at a serial killer," Beverly added. "One formidable psychopath!"

"Derrick believes aliens used a death ray—his way of explaining the condition of the bodies," Justin said.

"Sounds like Derrick," Beverly said. "You've never actually seen our murderous fiend's handiwork, have you?"

"Only read the descriptions in the paper," Justin said.

"I could almost believe Derrick's theory," Beverly said. "This is just too incredible!"

Beverly leaned back in her comfy chair to look at the ceiling. "If I remember correctly, you once made an unofficial call on our Medical Examiner, Leslie Graves."

"Um, yeah," Justin sheepishly replied. "Why?"

Justin remembered how upset Beverly was with him when he let that bit of information slip. But three months ago his clandestine visit to the coroner proved very helpful in stopping Siffer. Beverly eventually forgave him the impropriety. She surprised him with her next request!

"Go pay her another visit. See what angelic insights you can gather from her mind. See if you can glean anything off one of the bodies."

"You actually want me to go there?"

"It makes perfect sense for you to get more involved!" Beverly said.

Justin leaned forward in the chair, rubbing his temples. His facial expression took a nosedive. "Not again!" he moaned.

"Something unnatural—supernatural, is going on here," Beverly insisted. "Don't you see it?"

Justin just moaned.

****

Brian Cosgrove had no idea where he was or how he came to be passed out on some dirty hardwood floor. It was dark. His surroundings were run down and deserted. A couple of sparse rays of light penetrated the room through a partially soot-blackened window off to his right. As his eyes adjusted he looked around. What appeared to be birds, silhouetted in the darkness, hung from the ceiling overhead. More bird figures appeared mounted around the room as his eyes continued to adjust to the dark. There was a table cluttered with papers, books, and a globe in the center of the room.

Brian was on his back. He attempted to sit up only to have his head throb. Sitting made him woozy. It also made him sick to his stomach, so he lay back down to let it pass. A sickly-sweet odor lingered in his nostrils. Towering at his feet, a tall, ornately framed mirror rose to the ceiling in front of him. Reflected in the mirror he saw piles of boxes stacked by the wall behind him. With a few deep breaths, Brian attempted to sit again. Succeeding this time, he tried standing.

The floor swayed under him briefly. Regaining his balance to keep from falling over, he found himself facing the mirror. Something odd about this mirror caught his attention. He examined the reflection with fascination. It undulated, a trick of the eyes, he supposed, brought on by his current condition. The reflection rippled again, acting more like a reflection in a pool of water than a solid glass mirror. Brian temporarily lost his balance again. Taking a step backwards, he rubbed his eyes. He looked again.

A billowing blackness suddenly appeared at the back of the mirror. It swelled and grew like a storm cloud. Brian turned quickly to look behind him. Doing so hit him with a wave of nausea. Only the stacks of boxes remained there, silently stacked against the wall.

He turned back to the mirror. The blackness continued to grow. It now moved toward him. Again, Brian looked behind him. Still only boxes. The cloud began to ebb and flow, taking on form—a partial human shape! Frightened eyes now formed and stared back at Brian. Now a full face, the apparition's lips moved, mouthing unheard words. Brian just stood there, frozen.

All at once, the face of the old man dissolved back into the cloud, which quickly dispersed into the depths of the mirror. An undulating blue light now appeared in its stead. The light darted out from the mirror like a blue snake and struck Brian. It wrapped itself around him as an agonizing scream escaped Brian's throat. His face twisted and shrank, contorted beyond recognition. His eyes fell back into his skull, his body twisting, becoming shrunken, leathery. Dried up, hollowed leg bones snapped, bringing his body crashing to the floor in a heap. Immediately, the blue light darted back into the mirror and was gone.

From somewhere behind the shadows of the attic a voice whispered, "Ahh…good."

****

Detectives Henrycks and Selden suddenly found themselves shifted into high gear with the discovery of a third body—same condition as the first two with no identifying marks, no additional trace evidence, this was definitely the work of a mastermind serial killer. They had no way to determine means, or motive. The opportunity came during the night. The evidence pointed to the mansion as a possible location for at least one of the murders.

The remains of the newest victim were found in the early morning hours off of Route 51 in the weeds by the roadside. A motorist, stopping to repair a flat tire, lost his breakfast when he made the discovery. He immediately dialed 911. Detective Henrycks was the first to arrive on the scene.

By late afternoon, the coroner's office had identified the victim as one Brian Cosgrove, sixteen, of Angel Falls. The common factors of the case were clear. All the victims were male, about sixteen years of age, all attended Falls High School. The only breaks in the case came with the discovery of a single human hair on the first victim's body. DNA results on the hair were in—a match was found. This evidence corroborated another piece of evidence: two of the victims carried cell phones. The presence of fingerprints, other than those of the owners of these phones, belonged to the same individual who belonged to the hair: Charles Phillip Underwood!

Tom Selden was incredulous. "I know this kid! I sincerely doubt he could accomplish something like this!" he told Henrycks.

"The evidence points directly to the Underwood boy, all three victims were known to him. They went to his school!" Detective Henrycks explained. "I go by the evidence—it doesn't lie!"

Selden was insistent. "But where's the motive? The means? Look, even we can't figure out what happened to these boys—how on earth do you suppose a mere sixteen-year-old accomplished something so horrific?"

"I admit...it's got me stumped too, but it's all we have to go on!" Henrycks said. "But I'm told the kid's a genius—who knows what he might be capable of? It's possible he's working with someone!"

"Highly doubtful!" Tom replied. "The kid is smart but doesn't fit the profile of a serial killer!"

"Respectfully, Tom, I've seen some things you wouldn't believe! At least let me question the boy again."

Tom realized, procedurally, questioning was mandated. "Just question. I don't want charges brought at this time—keep looking for additional evidence. I'm sure it will clear him."

****

Detective Henrycks pulled his unmarked car to the curb in front of CPU's home and parked. As he lifted himself out of his car he happened to look down at the odometer: it had just turned over to exactly thirty-two-thousand miles. The number thirty-two seemed to amuse him. He smiled, closed the car door, and walked up to the Underwood's doorway. He knocked on the door and moments later a woman answered. She was in her early fifties, with a pleasant smile.

"Mrs. Underwood, I am Detective Jake Henrycks. I'd like you and your son, Charles, to come to the station please."

Mrs. Underwood's smile faded. "What is this about?"

"I just need to ask him a few additional questions related to classmates of his. You are required to be with him during questioning because of his age," Henrycks said.

Mrs. Underwood crossed her arms across her chest. "The classmates who died? Do you think my son is involved?"

"I only have questions for him at this time, Mrs. Underwood. Anything he knows about these classmates could help our investigation."

CPU's mom told the detective to wait outside while she collected her son and her coat. She closed the laptop she had been working on before the detective arrived and called her son.

CPU panicked. "Questions? What more could I possibly know?"

"Depends on what he asks—it shouldn't be too bad," his mom said in an effort to offer her son some comfort.

For CPU, the request to go to police headquarters came as a shock out of the blue. It reminded him of a day he went fishing in the bay with his dad. A snapper fish, fleeing from a predator, jumped right out of the water, smacking him right in the face. It was the only fish he caught on that fishing trip. This, too, felt like a sudden slap in the face.

Twenty minutes later CPU sat with his mom across a table from Henrycks in the interrogation room. Henrycks' questions bothered CPU. His first meeting with Henrycks was bad enough. A second trip to police headquarters alarmed him even more. Had he heard correctly? Did someone associate his name with the word 'accomplice'?

Henrycks, still wearing his winter coat, adjusted himself in his chair. He fumbled in his right coat pocket until he finally pulled something out.

CPU's mother gasped, vehemently protesting when Henrycks dropped several photos of the three victims down in front of them. CPU's scientific mind, however, while disgusted at first, found something fascinating in what he saw. He could not look away. Henrycks expected he might look away in disgust if he was innocent. Photos like these are difficult for most people to look at. But a killer might admire his work. He felt he had hit the jackpot seeing CPU's fixation on the victims.

"See something?" he asked CPU.

"I've seen this before!" CPU answered.

CPU's mom turned suddenly to face her son as she and the detective responded in unison, "You have!?"

Henrycks leaned forward. CPU's mom thought she was about to lose her son. One of them was disappointed, the other relieved.

"Well, yes," CPU said. "In horror movies where the victim's life force is drained away."

"Really! In a *movie*! Good night!" Henrycks objected.

Henrycks tried to impress upon CPU the seriousness of the predicament he was in. The hair, his fingerprints on the victim's cell phones, all pointed to his involvement one way or another. Plus, even though such evidence was circumstantial, all three victims were in his grade at school. One of them lived only a few houses away on his street. It did not look good for him!

"Your fingerprints were found on two of the victims' cell phones," Henrycks revealed. "How do you explain that?"

CPU only needed a second to realize the answer. "I've worked on those phones—it's my job!"

Henrycks cleared his throat and pulled a clear plastic baggie from his desk drawer. "See this? It's a human hair."

CPU could barely see the tiny object. "So?"

"It was found on the first victim—DNA tells us it belongs to you!"

Both mother and son looked at each other in unbelief.

Henrycks laid the baggie on the table in front of CPU. "It's the *only* thing found on the body. How'd it get there?"

"I have no idea!" CPU said. "I never spent time with the kid—I barely knew him. I certainly did not kill him!"

CPU's mom intervened. "I think this has gone far enough, detective! Are you actually planning to arrest my son?"

Henrycks could think of nothing further to ask the boy so he dismissed them both. Anxiety filled the car during the drive home. Mrs. Underwood attempted to ease her son's fears, explaining the detective was just doing his job. Although, in the back of her mind, nagging doubts caused her to wonder about the truth. Surely Henrycks knew her sixteen-year-old was incapable of doing the horrible things she saw in those pictures!

CPU's mind flew in every direction on the way home in an attempt to understand the impossibility of the situation he was in. Impossibility! Suddenly it came to him: these crimes *had* to be supernatural in origin! Only one person could fix this!

"I feel like I'm in a Stephen King movie!" CPU balked. "I need to see Justin!"

Instead of going directly home, Mrs. Underwood dropped her son off at the Thyme's home. She called to him not to be late for dinner, adding everything will turn out OK—not to worry.

Right.

"She's such a mom!" an embarrassed CPU told Justin, who answered the door.

"They all are—and good thing too!" Justin said. "Come on in!"

Derrick was also visiting Justin; he recognized the upset in CPU's face. He and Justin had been talking about the deaths of the three high school students before CPU arrived. They were shocked when CPU confided about being interrogated again by Henrycks at police headquarters.

Derrick wanted to say, "I hope you like bread and water!" but decided against it. His friend looked really, really upset.

The three of them sat on the couch in the Thyme's living room. CPU asked Justin for a favor. He wanted to prove to everyone in the room he was not involved in any wrongdoing. He proposed Justin read him so no one had any doubts whatsoever! He also wanted him to get inside Henrycks' head. Justin was hesitant.

"You know it's not necessary," Justin said. "You haven't done anything!"

"For everyone's peace of mind—even my own, please!" CPU said.

"But why Henrycks?"

"He scares me!" CPU said.

"He's a cop—just doing his job!" Derrick insisted. Justin agreed.

CPU gave all his reasons why Henrycks should be checked out. Justin reluctantly consented to his requests, if only to calm him down. First, his creepy stare told CPU the man was up to something. Next, he saw Henrycks with the most recent victim earlier that week. Justin and Derrick both explained, or tried, that cops are not gentle at their jobs. There's a lot at stake and getting to the truth sometimes gets uncomfortable. Apparently what they said made sense as far as Henrycks was concerned, but CPU still wanted to be examined by Justin.

"OK, bud. Look at me," Justin instructed CPU.

"Will this hurt?" CPU asked.

Derrick leaned in closer to CPU. "Ever have brain freeze, Chuck?" Derrick asked. "Like when you eat those frozen fudgsicles?"

Justin shoved him away. "No, Derrick. He won't feel a thing! In fact, it's done!"

"Wow, that was quick!" CPU said. "What did you see?"

"All your upset and your anxiety—nothing unexpected!"

"Yeah, but what else?"

"What you got Derrick for his birthday," Justin smiled.

"C'mon, what else?" CPU whined.

Derrick got excited. "What'd he get me, Justin?"

"Nothing, Derrick—I was kidding." He turned to CPU, "Like I already expected, you're clean!"

"I guess there is no need to check Henrycks," CPU said.

"Look, I'm supposed to meet Tom and Beverly later today at headquarters. I'll do it if it will make you feel better," Justin said. "But I doubt I'll find a problem there."

"I know," CPU said. "But thanks."

Derrick shook his little buddy by the shoulders. "You're just in shock from being questioned by the big, scary detective!"

CPU pulled away and glared at Derrick. "Knock it off!"

******

Justin knew Beverly wanted him to reveal his angelic secret to Tom! He understood Beverly's reasons, but it still made him uncomfortable. 'More' did not make 'merrier.' When she hid the supernatural elements surrounding Siffer's demise from Tom it felt like she betrayed him. But under the circumstances, in order to protect Justin, some details at the time needed to be covered up. This time she wanted Tom to be prepared ahead of time. Let the detective do his job and deal with the final results! Working successfully with Tom would require full disclosure.

Justin conceded to her argument. If Angel Falls is ground zero for supernormal events Tom should come onboard now. Besides, hiding things from Tom exhausted her, while working outside purely legal boundaries offered Justin no small degree of discomfort.

Tom was a decent guy—Justin felt certain of it, even without having read him. Plus, he, Beverly, and Tom would be a formidable trio to oppose any adversary, supernatural or not! With Tom in the know, Justin may even be able to convince him of CPU's complete innocence, which would allow them to concentrate on finding the real guilty party.

Chapter 7

From beyond Visitation Lake in the west, a lone figure emerged from the woods. He moved eastward toward the waterfall. Adorned in brilliant white garb, his shoulder-length hair flowed with the gentle breeze and the cadence of his steps. The splendor of the lake struck a peaceful chord deep within his entire being. Upon reaching the eastern edge of the plateau, he surveyed the bustling town in the valley below.

Light mist from the waterfall, the pounding of the water on rocks below, refreshed him. His mouth formed a smile as he remembered a time when there existed no liveliness of spirit below. That time marked a prior visit to the area on behalf of the One Who rules all things. Now, an important mission was before him. It would be his last visit to this place, this Angel Falls. Even the town's name brought a glint of delight to his eyes.

He raised his voice, hands held high, and spoke towards those below, now going about their lives unaware of his existence. No one heard his declaration, but *their* hearing was not the point. It was a testimony for the ages. He addressed an audience of One. "By Alastair Alda's act of faith this city, at death's door, has been made whole once again."

Having spoken these words he turned back toward the woods and disappeared.

****

Contrary to the song, the weather outside was not frightful. With a warming trend forecast for the next few days, his friends being in school or at work, Justin took this time to relax on a park bench. He read a book. It was like spring in November. The temperature reached sixty-seven degrees with no wind to create a wind-chill factor. Not a cloud could be seen overhead, allowing the sun to shine in all its glory. A light jacket was all Justin needed to stay comfortable.

He took a momentary break from his reading to look around the park. Mothers with babies and children too young for preschool occupied all the remaining park benches. The women gathered in groups to discuss, he supposed, child rearing, their husbands, or anything else that crossed a young mother's mind. Some of them may be discussing plans to return to work once their children reached preschool age. None of them, however, realized the full extent of the peril besetting Angel Falls at this very moment. Of that he was certain.

News reports of a serial killer at large seemed not to concern these moms. First, the reports made it known these deaths occurred at night. Secondly, the killer was only interested in teenage males. Finally, there was strength in numbers. No one would dare attempt to harm this band of momma bears in full daylight! However, the unnatural circumstances surrounding these events were completely lost on the population. There was no guarantee a demon's modus operandi—assuming a demon is involved—wouldn't suddenly change.

Justin felt a little guilty enjoying himself in the sun while CPU stressed about being a person of interest in these crimes. Extraordinary intelligence tended to make his young friend rather high strung. CPU was a year ahead of others his age scholastically, almost three years younger than Justin and Derrick, but smaller than most kids even his own age. The Underwood boy behaved more maturely than many his age. But every now and then the round-rimmed, spectacled Harry Potter look-alike acted like a naive child.

Derrick always had a conspiracy theory to explain the unexplainable. CPU leaned on science. Derrick normally presented a bold front in the face of danger, CPU was more fearful. But Justin had to admit CPU showed enormous courage a few months ago when he faced killer security guards at GenEx

Labs. He proved to be a great asset when they defeated Siffer!

Justin thought back to the time when he first met Charles Phillip Underwood. It was actually Derrick who first became friends with CPU. This was a time, two years ago, before Justin knew either one of them. Derrick, a sophomore, was working on a paper in the high school computer lab. The lab accommodated twenty students at a time (there were twenty computers in the lab): ten Windows PCs and ten iMacs. Derrick's Windows computer was giving him trouble, making it difficult for him to get his paper done.

There were four other students besides Derrick in the lab on that day. Three of those students had become more interested in tormenting a younger fourth student who, as a result, was having little success getting his work done. Derrick was a big guy, a sports jock; he was also very intelligent (which his silly conspiracy theories failed to demonstrate).

As Derrick became more irritated with the lab computer he was working on, the distraction created by the bullies at the next table put him over the edge! When the three tormentors started to drag the boy to the restroom to give him a 'swirlie' Derrick took action.

He jumped up from his seat, slid across the table behind him and grabbed the first offender. He picked him up and tossed out of the lab. He punched the bully who had the young CPU by the arm in the stomach. The kid released his grip on CPU, jumped the table, and flew out of the lab. Derrick turned to face the final attacker whose facial expression suddenly turned to dread. He ran out of the room as fast as he could.

"Thanks," the young boy said.

"No problem," Derrick replied. "Three against one doesn't suit me much."

"Maybe now I can get something done," the young man said.

Derrick walked back to his computer. "I wish I could. You don't know anything about these electronic pains in the butt, do you?"

"Sure do, how can I help?"

Derrick demonstrated the problem he was having. The young CPU sat in front of the monitor while his fingers flew across the keyboard. Soon the PC was responding normally! Derrick retook his seat, the mouse, and keyboard.

"Thanks! You're pretty handy with these things!" Derrick said. "I'm Derrick, by the way. What name does my computer whiz friend go by?"

CPU collected his books and started to leave for his next class. "Charles. But you can call me CPU."

"Wait! Before you go, what do I do if this computer acts up again?" Derrick asked.

"Use one of the iMacs!" CPU said with a grin and walked out the door.

For the remainder of the school year, Derrick and CPU spent time together at lunch. They'd talk about sports, computers, school, and God, among many other things. As their friendship grew, no one ever bullied Charles Phillip Underwood again. At least, that's the version of the story Derrick told Justin.

It wasn't until a few weeks later when Justin met Derrick and CPU for the first time. He met them at church. After some urging from his parents to get back into the habit, Justin finally attended a Sunday school class following the service. When it was over everyone congregated outside by the parking lot to meet and greet. It was there Justin bumped into Derrick and CPU. The strength of Derrick's and CPU's faith was obvious, while Justin had questions. In spite of this, or because of it, the three hit it off. Over the next couple of years they became fast friends, with Derrick occasionally explaining the church services to Justin, who continued to attend.

Of course, Justin's recent experiences with his angelic powers did much toward growing his faith. In fact, the three boys' faith eventually became the strongest tie which bound them together.

Justin's reverie into the past ended abruptly. Someone sat next to him on the park bench. A man dressed all in white, taking in the activities in the park, looked over at him and smiled.

"Quite the nice day, yes Justin?" the stranger in white said.

"Do I know you?" Justin asked, feeling a bit uneasy.

"You do, and you do not," the stranger said.

"Excuse me? Who are you?"

The stranger shifted his body on the park bench in order to face Justin directly. "I have a message for you: 'Be strong, and let your heart take courage, all you who wait on the Lord!'"

Justin looked at him with growing curiosity. "Your quoting from the Psalms."

"You still show reluctance to act," the stranger continued. "You must face your fears!"

"Who are you; how do you know my name?"

"I am Micah, an archangel. You could say I am your parent, of sorts. The celestial abilities you possess within you come from me."

Justin, wide-eyed, inched his way down the bench, away from the stranger.

"You have no reason to be afraid, Justin," Micah responded. "Trust your gift!"

"I never asked for this!" Justin protested.

"You are an overcomer!"

Justin poised himself to jump off the bench, ready to run. "If it's a gift, why am I so afraid of it?"

The angel's next words astonished Justin. "Mine was the wrongdoing. But the LORD who, by His Sovereignty, can take what is evil and bring about good. The battle is the LORD's; He has prepared you!"

Justin considered the angel's words. This was how God worked in the case of Joseph, being sold as a slave into Egypt. Joseph's brothers meant to harm him. God used Joseph to save Egypt from a severe famine. "All things work together for good…."

An angel, acting wrongly, did this to him! Really?

Now suddenly more curious than fearful, Justin asked, "Battle? Who, or what, is this enemy?"

"In time these things will present themselves."

Justin's frustration with riddles grew into anger. "But nothing's clear; Siffer was easy to spot— here there's nothing to go on!"

"Remember from Whom your true strength comes," is all Micah would say. Then, for mere seconds, the angel radiated with sudden, luminous white light, and vanished.

Justin breathed a heavy sigh. He could feel his heart racing in his chest, his shaking hands and arms felt weak. Collapsing back on the bench, he tried to wrap his swimming head around what just happened. He just met a real angel—*his* angel! Fear, once again, flooded his heart. What was the nature of this new enemy? Who, what, and where was he; would he be prepared?

****

Still in shock, Justin sought out his friends, eager to share with them what just happened in the park. Finally connecting via cell phones, they decided to meet up at the lake as long as the weather held up. Fortunately, the sunny skies continued. According to the latest weather report it would remain sunny for the next two days. The lake, his favorite spot, always afforded a respite from stress.

He drove his Civic to his destination. Derrick drove himself, taking CPU along with him. Turning onto a southern access road to the top of the plateau, Derrick arrived two minutes after Justin. He parked his car next to the Honda, where Justin waited listening to the radio. He exited his vehicle with a signal to walk with him to the willow tree near the falls.

Without the breeze, there was little mist drifting back from the waterfall. Whatever snow there had been had vanished under sunny skies. They took their usual positions on the now dry ground under the willow. In spite of the warmer conditions, CPU noticed Justin's hands trembled slightly.

"You OK? Why are we here?" CPU asked.

"You cold?" Derrick asked. "Maybe we should go back."

"No, I'm not cold—just overwhelmed!" Justin explained. "My angel visited me in the park today!"

"I don't get it; *who* was this?" Derrick asked.

CPU livened up. "*Your* angel? The one you got your--"

"Yes! The one who turned me into what I am!" Justin snapped. "He wanted to warn me; something is about to go down!"

"Another Sifferism?" Derrick asked.

"Exactly." Justin answered. He calmed a little but his response was grave. "And—it's close."

"But is this angel gonna help us—help *you*?" Derrick wanted to know.

"Nope! Just kinda said it's gonna be OK." Justin said. "Then he vanished."

"Is this the angel who saved Grangeville?" CPU asked.

"He called himself Micah—one of the archangels."

"Did you get his autograph?" Derrick asked.

"Don't be stupid! He's an angel! What would I do with an autograph?"

Derrick thought a moment. "Sell it on eBay?"

CPU and Justin both groaned.

"Sorry," Derrick said. "I'm not sure how to deal with something like this!"

The three sat for a while in silence, staring at the few clouds floating overhead. CPU was the first to bring up what Derrick was also wondering. "An actual angel comes to you and that was *all* you talked about?"

"I'd like to see just how coherent you'd be!" Justin objected.

"I would've asked him for next season's football scores!" Derrick said.

"You would have fallen over in a dead faint!" CPU chided him.

"Forget it guys! His message was simple. 'Be encouraged'!"

"I would have had some theology questions for him," CPU said.

Justin closed his eyes and leaned back against the tree. "At the time it never crossed my mind."

"So, are you?" Derrick asked.

Justin looked at him, "Am I what?"

"Encouraged! Are you ready?"

Good question. He might be feeling a bit better now that his friends were part of this. But he felt far from being ready for something of angelic proportions! This unearthly visitor's words replayed in his mind. "Be encouraged!" What reason was there for encouragement? Even Beverly said, "get involved!" Could these be the indications of a sign from above? After all, what more authentications do the words from an *angel* need? At that moment, Justin steeled his mind. He settled his emotions. Whatever was to come, he would force himself to be ready for it!

Chapter 8

Upon hearing one of his New Horizons customers, Jeb Wechsler, had become very ill, CPU decided to pay him a visit. Not because he had any warm feelings for the old codger. Wechsler's manner made warming up to him difficult, for sure. Something inside CPU made him feel sad for the guy. But there was something more. Wechsler's cryptic warning, spoken last time he was with him, had haunted him. CPU knew a certain amount of paranoia sometimes comes with old age. However, recent events—especially Justin's recent visitation— told him in this particular case, Wechsler probably sensed something real.

CPU was about to knock on Wechsler's door when it opened suddenly as someone rushed past him, almost knocking him over. The man turned, quickly excused himself, then hurried off. The man's face was familiar, but CPU could not remember where he had seen him. Wechsler's door remained open, so CPU called in.

"Mr. Wechsler, CPU here. Are you up for a visit?"

There was no answer at first. Then a faint moan followed by a weak, "Back here!"

Wechsler, bedridden, called for CPU to come on in. He shut the front door and walked through the living room to the bedroom located toward the back of the cottage. Breathing became difficult; the cottage was stuffy and hot. As he passed Wechsler's desk he noticed the man's laptop. It was turned off, but the lid was open—quite unlike the paranoid habits of its owner.

CPU closed the laptop, then noticed the thermostat was set to a stifling ninety degrees. Elderly like it warm, but this was too much! Charles turned down the thermostat to a more comfortable seventy-eight, which he remembered it being set to on his last visit. Wechsler was laying down; he could barely motion CPU to come into the room.

"Who was that Mr. Wechsler?" CPU asked.

"That doctor—Craven," Wechsler answered and coughed several times.

"Was this a house call?" CPU asked.

"A rare occurrence," Wechsler wheezed.

"What's this doctor doing for you, Mr. Wechsler?"

"Not much," Wechsler pointed to the night stand next to his bed. "Just these pills."

"You look like you need an ambulance," CPU said. "Didn't Doctor Craven think so?"

"He don't...seem like...much...of a doc," Wechsler said between hacking coughs. CPU noted the wheeze in Wechsler's labored breathing was not a good sign. "The doc came by a week ago. I wasn't so bad then. He just keeps givin' me pills."

CPU looked at the bottle of pills. The label said only, "For Blood Pressure." He took out a capsule and opened it, giving it a sniff. Dabbing some of the contents onto his finger he took a taste. CPU had no idea what he expected, he only saw this done on murder mystery TV shows. He decided to take the pill to have it examined. After gently sliding the capsule back together, he shoved it into his pocket.

"Mr. Wechsler, when did you last use your laptop?"

"Haven't. Not since you fixed it up," Wechsler said.

CPU noted that was two weeks ago. "Anyone besides the doctor been in to see you since then?"

"Not a soul!" Wechsler coughed. "Spent most of the time here in bed!"

Two weeks ago CPU had closed up the laptop, so who opened it since then, if not Wechsler? Leaving the answer to that question for another time, CPU felt it more important to move quickly on the matter of Wechsler's medication. Maybe Justin would know what to do. He bid Wechsler feel better and left. If Wechsler's only other visitor had been the doctor, what possible reason would Dr. Craven have to be into his laptop?

****

Justin prepared to meet with Tom and Beverly. Afterwards, he would visit the Coroner, Leslie Graves. He hoped to use his 'special sense' to get something to jump out at him. Maybe if he viewed the bodies or read Graves' emotional state he might accomplish his goal. Anything to help solve these murders! Before leaving, his friend insisted on his help. CPU explained Wechsler's condition.

Justin curiously eyed the blood pressure pill CPU handed him. They devised a plan to have Justin impose a suggestion on Leslie's mind, a desire to examine the pill. As far as seeing Leslie again, only one thing concerned Justin. He sort of made a fool of himself the first time he met her. He hoped she had forgotten the incident.

****

Selden sat in his office, door closed, when Justin and Beverly appeared outside, They looked in and waved. Selden motioned them to come in, which they did, Beverly closing the door behind her.

"What's with the clandestine meet-up, Bev?" Selden asked.

"You remember Justin, don't you?" she asked.

"The photographer? Yes, I remember," Selden replied. He shook Justin's hand. "How've you been, Justin?"

"Doin' OK, I suppose."

Selden offered the two of them a seat across from his desk. "OK. So, what's this all about?"

Beverly began, "Tom, I need you to keep an open mind."

"You have another outrageous theory about the case we're working on?" Tom asked.

"Not quite. This isn't about the case; it's about Justin," she said. "But on a related note, you may find this case is more 'outrageous' than you realize."

Tom looked over at Justin who sat there looking down at his hands folded in his lap. Joking, he asked, "He's not here to confess, is he?"

"Please, Tom, I'm serious! Shut up and listen!" Beverly bristled.

Tom suddenly became apologetic. "Sorry, Bev. What's got you so worked up?"

"What I'm about to tell you is for you *only*, no one else—and it's unbelievable! When I first learned what I'm about to reveal to you I didn't believe it either!" she said.

Tom shifted uneasily in his chair. "C'mon, Bev. I'm too weary for a walk down crazy street!"

"Before you throw us out, just listen for a minute," she pleaded.

Tom shook his head. "I'm telling you..."

"You're a good Catholic boy. Do you believe in angels?" she asked him.

"Sure, I suppose. So what?"

"What happened to Siffer—who and what he was—plays a part in all this," Beverly continued.

"Siffer…. You almost died at his hand," Tom said softly. "How is he involved? What's this got to do with Justin?"

"Ever heard of the Nephilim?" she asked.

"Old Testament stuff—the progeny of angels and humans—what of it?" Selden replied.

"Angel Falls. You know how it got its name?" she asked.

Tom shifted his weight in his chair again and wondered where she was going with this. "Yeah, I know the legend. Something about Angels supposedly saved this place hundreds of years ago?"

"But it isn't fiction—through one of the angels there arose a Nephilim—who added his genetic nature to our gene pool!"

"Bev, maybe I sort of believe in angels but this…." Tom looked over at Justin, who now looked up to make eye contact with him. "Wait a minute...you're saying *he's* this angelic thing?"

"Not a *thing*, but yes. His DNA is mingled with that of a Nephilim. And some very special powers go with it," she said. "Tom, I've *seen* it for myself!"

Beverly explained Siffer had the same gene. His supernatural powers would have destroyed Angel Falls, were it not for Justin.

Tom shook his head. "What have you seen? Beverly, what's happened to you?"

"It's all real, Tom. The Grangeville angels, angelic powers. Siffer's powers were demonic; Justin defeated Siffer with these same powers!"

"I thought nanobots burned Siffer out of existence! Isn't that why no body was found—you were my eyewitness!"

Beverly realized it would take more than words to convince her friend. "You need to know the whole truth, Tom." She turned to Justin and winked. "Let's give him a small sample of your abilities, like the one you once pulled on me!"

Justin nodded.

Tom looked back and forth between Justin and Beverly. "What's going on?"

"Brace yourself, buddy!" she said.

Suddenly, there was a knock on Tom's office door. When Tom signaled for the newcomer to enter, the door opened. Another Justin stood in the doorway, grinning. "I'd ask to come in, but I see I already am," the copy at the door said.

Tom gasped. He looked at Justin who sat across from him then at the Justin in the doorway and nearly fell off his seat. Immediately, the copy disappeared and Justin—the real one sitting opposite Tom—said, "That rattled Beverly!"

"What… what just happened?" Tom choked.

"Justin can do a lot more," Beverly explained. "What I'm getting at is he can help us with our latest horror story."

"Because we're not dealing with your everyday kind of case!" Justin added.

Tom looked at Justin. "You're for *real*? Some kind of angel-powered superhero? How many others know about this?"

"Just the three of us and my two friends, Derrick and CPU," Justin said. "And let's keep it at that."

Tom needed a few more minutes to warm up to this startling revelation. There was just a little comfort knowing Beverly was in on this. However, he felt a bit miffed she hadn't told him sooner. He always thought Justin was a good kid; Beverly always spoke highly of him. But his respect for this eighteen-year-old now turned into fear. Powers like this in the wrong kind of person would be Angel Falls' worst nightmare. And today he learned Siffer had been just such a nightmare. Maybe Bev was right to hide it from him!

Tom did not know Derrick, but, of course, CPU was another issue. Did being Justin's friend seal his innocence? Still, if CPU was his friend, it created a problem.

Changing the subject, Tom informed them, "We've had to bring CPU in for questioning. Some disturbing evidence with his name on it came to our attention recently."

"Justin can also get a reading of people's emotions and intents," Beverly cut in.

"Like reading their minds?" Tom asked.

"Not quite, but a close second—and very helpful in cases like these," Justin said. "I can tell you, CPU did nothing wrong!"

"You're not seriously considering a sixteen-year-old boy for these murders, are you Tom?" Beverly asked.

"Me? Not really. Not too sure about Henrycks. It's just, well, there's no way for him to completely ignore some stark evidence!"

"Henrycks is sure in a pickle!" Beverly said. "I can relate—but Justin can vouch for his friend."

"That reminds me," Justin said. "I'd like to meet Detective Henrycks."

Beverly and Justin could see Tom was still bewildered by the evidence—the evidence concerning Justin's secret, that is. He was having some trouble organizing his thoughts, his hands still trembled. Beverly offered to discuss the matter with him further at a later date, perhaps over lunch. Tom agreed and offered to take both of them to meet Henrycks. Like Justin, Beverly had yet to meet him. She welcomed the opportunity. As a reporter, keeping open lines of communication with the police department was vital. It made her job as a reporter much easier.

Before the three of them left Tom's office to meet Henrycks, Justin took a quick look into Tom's eyes. He never had the chance to read him so he took this moment for an opportunity to do so. No red flags presented themselves. Here was a man of integrity. Now it was time to see what kind of stuff this other detective was made of.

On the way to Henrycks' desk, Beverly warned Tom again: no one else was to know of Justin's true nature. Tom saw the wisdom of the request and committed to keeping Justin's identity safe. As they approached Henrycks, Henrycks, still wearing his long winter coat, saw them coming and stood to greet them.

Introductions were made along with a bit of small talk. Henrycks was amiable but his stern, business-like manner made an exact reading difficult. But, as far as he could tell, Henrycks also seemed an honorable man—but he had his quirks. For one thing, Justin picked up on his tendency to be a bit superstitious. Henrycks always kept thirty-two cents in newly minted coins in his front pants pocket. There were other quirky, vague issues floating around in Henrycks' brain, which Justin dismissed as personal idiosyncrasies.

Their discussion quickly turned toward speculation about CPU. Justin was politely adamant his friend was not involved. Beverly backed his assertion claiming complete confidence in Justin's ability to know people, especially those close to him. Tom Selden said very little. Rather, he listened with interest at their three-way conversation.

Henrycks admitted to being stumped by this case, mostly by the victims themselves. It was unfathomable how three healthy teenagers turned up the way they did. He felt compelled to look further into the evidence, but, based on the most recent evidence, there was no way he could remove CPU from his list of suspects.

"I'm not supposed to discuss the case, but your friend is not my only suspect," Henrycks admitted.

Tom assured Beverly and Justin, "We are still gathering evidence. This case is far from over!"

Beverly suggested Henrycks avail himself of Justin's help. She cited Justin's success in solving one of Angel Falls' more recent horror stories. Based on what he just witnessed, Tom cautiously backed her assertion.

"You missed the 'Case of the Mad Scientist,'" Tom told Henrycks. "Justin was instrumental in solving that one."

"He's young, but extremely competent," Beverly added. "He won't get in your way."

Henrycks, who preferred to work alone, politely said he'd think about it. Having much work to do, he suddenly dismissed himself. Tom, likewise, went back to work, so Beverly left with Justin. On their way out of the building, an idea popped into Beverly's head unrelated to the current mystery. "Justin, it's about time I start using your photographic talents for more than fluff pieces," she said. "A photojournalist with your excellent detective instincts would be an asset to the newspaper."

Justin grinned.

****

"If you're heading out to the morgue now, don't forget this," CPU said. He handed Justin one of Wechsler's pills.

"Mr. Wechsler's in pretty poor condition. I'll imprint 'rush' on the ME's mind," Justin assured his friend.

As he drove to the morgue, Justin's mind drifted back to his first encounter with Leslie Graves. She had a quick wit and an odd sense of humor. She was also a very skilled, competent medical examiner. But, was that enough? This case probably had Graves as baffled as everyone else. By its very supernatural nature he wondered how successful merely human attempts to solve it could be. Who, or what, had the power necessary to pull off these horrific slaughters? Would his unusual abilities be enough to figure any of this out?

He brought along his 'press pass.' It was the same one he used last time to worm his way into Graves' lab and into her good graces. The pass dangled around his neck, swaying back and forth, as he approached her office. Only one of the three bodies remained—the last victim, and it looked like she was finishing up her examination.

Justin's rather sheepish knock at the lab entrance perked the ME right up.

"My goodness, Mr. Thyme from the Trib! What brings you by?"

So she did remember.

"Looks like you've been busy, Mrs. Graves," Justin said. He pointed to the body on the table. "Those three students who were killed, is that one of them?"

"First, I told you last time we met to call me Leslie!" she said. "And yes, he's one! If you want to take a closer look," she pointed to the other side of the lab, "remember: my sink is over by that wall!"

Normally, the Coroner would not allow just anyone into her lab. But this boy had a press pass. Besides, she liked his photographic work in the Falls Tribune. And he was so polite!

"I remember," Justin smiled. The last time he witnessed a corpse on Leslie's table he threw up in that sink. As he walked closer to the body, no creeping sensations, no premonitions or explosive visions overcame him. Fortunately, any grossness he once felt about the morgue must have lessened because his stomach, so far, held its own.

"Darnedest thing!" Leslie said as she watched Justin examine the corpse. "I first surmised this to be a case of exposure—exposure one might experience in outer space, sans spacesuit. But that's clearly ridiculous! I was grasping at straws by that time!" She laughed.

In actuality, this freeze-dried look might be what someone *would* look like after being exposed to the ravages of outer space. But how did anyone manage that? Continuing his examination, Justin noted the body had no unusual aroma except common to one after sitting in a morgue for several days. It almost looked as if someone made a

Styrofoam model of an Area 51 alien. Maybe the three victims did have an encounter with outer space!

Justin hesitatingly touched the body. To do so unnoticed, he entered Leslie's mind to distract her. He put on a rubber glove and gingerly examined the remains. Even through the glove, his touch suddenly generated a powerful response in his psyche. First, an eerie response—a defiled wave of malevolent energy struck him. Then a physical response—a tingling sensation shooting up and down his arm and spine! Justin jerked back his hand, lost the connection to Leslie, and stumbled backward.

"Everything all right, hon?" Leslie asked. "You look a little peaked."

Justin laughed it off. "Uh, fine! I thought something moved—some imagination, huh?"

"This place'll do it to ya," Leslie admitted.

Regaining his composure, Justin asked, "You found a human hair on the first victim?"

"Had to use a fine-toothed comb to get the hair—pun intended," she said and laughed. "It didn't show up during my initial examination."

Having looked into her mind, Justin realized Leslie had some serious doubts about her findings. Capitalizing on that fact he continued to question her. "Is it possible the hair could have been planted?" he asked.

"Not sure how, but it did cross my mind," she said. "Although, we're pretty tight here with security."

"Was there any time this room was left unattended?" Justin asked, still working from impressions received from Leslie's mind moments ago.

Leslie appeared a little uncomfortable as she thought back to that night. "I had my assistant close up for me," she said. "Now that you mention it, the lab might have been unsupervised for a minute or two."

Another bit of information from Leslie's mind. "You also had a visitor?"

"Why yes, I did! But he left the building before I did. Some doctor from New Horizons. I doubt...."

With the mention of New Horizons, Justin immediately knew who the doctor was.

"Thanks, Mrs. Graves, Uh, Leslie. You've been a great help!"

Looking directly into Leslie's eyes, Justin entered a final suggestion: *"analyze this pill and put a rush on it!"* He handed her a zip-loc baggie with the pill inside.

"I'll get right on it!" she said taking the baggie. "Thanks for stopping by Mr. Thyme! I'll be in touch."

Chapter 9

Justin, Derrick, and CPU walked up to the front door of the Cosgrove's home. CPU wanted to offer condolences on the death of Brian. Although he was not very close to Brian he felt obligated. They were classmate and neighbors. When Brian's mother answered the door the boys made their introductions.

Mrs. Cosgrove immediately thanked CPU for visiting her father during his illness. A sudden shock of understanding shot through CPU. Wechsler and Brian Cosgrove were related!

Mrs. Cosgrove held back tears and said, "Brian visited his grandfather to wish him well. The next day my son went missing."

Derrick stumbled for words, "I'm, I mean we, um...your son...uh, Brian. I mean we are very sorry...for your loss, Mrs. Cosgrove."

Justin nodded in agreement. "Yes," CPU added.

"I might lose dad next," Mrs. Cosgrove said, teary-eyed. "He seems to be on the decline."

The boys said they had Mr. Wechsler in their prayers, but CPU said nothing about his suspicions concerning her dad's treatment at the retirement center. He decided to bring it up on their walk back to Justin's place. As it turned out, they walked home in silence.

Once at Justin's, sitting in his living room, an emotional 'second wind' got the friends talking. There was no word yet from the coroner about Wechsler's pill. CPU described his last visit to Jeb Wechsler, how his condition grew progressively worse. He mentioned running into Doctor Craven just as he got there.

"Somebody tampered with Wechsler's laptop," CPU stated. "I think it was that doctor!"

"You're not being too overly suspicious, are you?" Derrick asked.

"I know I have seen this doctor somewhere— I just cannot figure out where!" CPU said. "I think that doctor was on Wechsler's laptop."

"But you didn't actually see him on it, right?" Derrick asked. "It's all circumstantial—you're quick to jump to conclusions!"

"Craven does seem to keep popping up," Justin suggested. "Although I can't for the life of me understand what he'd want with Mr. Wechsler's laptop!"

At that moment, Justin noticed the blinking red light on the answering machine in the kitchen telling him there was a message waiting. Justin hopped up from his chair, ran to the kitchen, and hit 'play.'

When the message finished playing, CPU looked at Derrick. "That clinches it!" he said. "I'm not paranoid after all!"

Derrick's stunned facial expression said it all. "Lead and traces of rat poison! His pills were actually poisoned!"

"We have to get Wechsler to stop taking those pills!" Justin said.

"Tom Selden needs to know what we know about the New Horizons physician!" CPU insisted.

"Still jumping to conclusions, Chuck!" Derrick said.

"He's right about one thing," Justin said. "We should let our detective friend know about the pill tampering!"

****

Justin plowed his Honda through traffic with an unspoken urgency. Derrick and CPU insisted three times he slow down. When they arrived at Wechsler's cottage unscathed, CPU jumped out of the car and pounded on the door. No lights were on; no one answered. He pounded on the door again. Derrick tried his shoulder against the locked door to no avail.

Justin listened. "Wait—hold on guys!" He grabbed the doorknob with his left hand and closed his eyes. His hand emitted a yellow glow when the three of them heard the doorknob go 'click.' The door opened!

"That's a *lot* easier than going through the door," Justin explained.

They quickly made their way inside; Derrick searched for a light switch and hit the lights.

"Quickly, Justin—he's back here!" CPU called.

Wechsler, barely breathing, only moaned when CPU called his name.

"I'm calling an ambulance!" Derrick said. "And the cops!"

Justin and CPU helped Wechsler sit up. He wheezed heavily and coughed, which seemed to clear his lungs up a bit allowing him to breathe just a little easier. When the MedTrans service arrived they carried Wechsler out. Justin informed a red-haired, ponytailed EMT of Wechsler's condition. She questioned the basis for his diagnosis. Immediately, CPU handed the EMT the bottle of Wechsler's pills (making sure he kept some for himself, in case he needed them later).

"Check these out!" CPU told her. "You'll see!"

"We're working with the police department," Justin added. "We have reason to believe Mr. Wechsler was slowly being poisoned."

Now they had a new piece to this puzzle. Fitting the pieces together into a coherent picture would not be easy. Why Brian, why Jeb Wechsler? CPU now realized Wechsler's alarm about New Horizons carried some weight. But was his doctor at the center of his fears, or someone else? What reason would Craven have for poisoning Wechsler or killing his grandson unless he was covering up something? More confusing, what was their relationship to the first victim, Alex? The motive also escaped them. One thing seemed clear: The killer, or killers attempted to make CPU their scapegoat.

The real kicker, discovering a weapon, presented a bigger problem. Nothing existed on earth that could do the things done to those students! Derrick's alien ray gun almost made sense! It momentarily occurred to the boys they might be dealing with the quintessential Mad Scientists. The mental picture gave them the chills.

****

Detective Selden asked to see Justin the next day. No explanation for meeting him was given, but there was an urgency in his voice. Justin gripped the steering wheel tightly as he sped his way to police headquarters. At one point he almost missed a stop sign. One rear wheel hopped the curb as he took one turn too sharply. He landed back in the road with a thump. Realizing he was getting reckless, he determined to slow the car and his breathing.

The meeting might be about the murders. Perhaps it involved disclosing something about his friendship with CPU. Maybe Selden had new issues with Justin's true nature. He wished Beverly was with him.

Once downtown, Justin pulled into a parking garage only two blocks from the station. He walked the two blocks briskly, prompted primarily by the twenty degree temperature, but also by a desire to hurry this meeting along. Being a brighter, sunnier day encouraged him but a little. He and Beverly had established a good working dynamic. He wondered if he and Tom Selden would be able to do the same.

Inside the three-story police headquarters, Justin took an elevator to the third floor. Upon his arrival, Tom greeted him cordially and offered him something to drink. Justin chose the coffee. After a couple of sips and a minute or two, he began to relax a bit. Once seated in Tom's office, Tom explained what he knew of the case so far.

"We now understand how your friend's fingerprints got on the two cell phones," Tom said. "But the most incriminating evidence is still the hair.

Whatever killed our victims virtually sanitized their bodies. One hair becomes patently obvious, but ultimately curious."

"The ME says someone could have found a way into her exam room and planted the hair," Justin said.

"You spoke to the ME?" Tom asked.

"Yeah. Me and her go back a ways."

"Right—a whole three months. Bev told me about your escapades. Did she actually *tell* you in those very words?" Tom asked.

"Well, after I checked out her state of mind. She had some doubts, so I asked her about them," Justin said. "So yes, I did ask her. That's what she'd been concerned about."

Tom's expression revealed his growing frustration. "OK. So now we have more questions than answers!"

"But it should clear CPU. I know he didn't do it!"

"Right. Your mind reading thing," Tom said. "Evidence is evidence. Between that and your skills, I'm more comfortable with hard evidence. Look at it this way: it's a little far-fetched to think anyone had access to CPU's head."

But not impossible. Still, Justin had no answer for him. He simply knew what he knew. Deciding to shift gears, Justin tried to tie in the

Wechsler poisoning. Tom questioned the relevancy of Wechsler's relationship to one of the victims. No relationship between Wechsler's poisoning and the murders existed in Tom's mind. Furthermore, only circumstantial evidence put Craven as the one who poisoned Wechsler! From there, it required an even greater leap to tie Craven to these murders. Based on Justin's 'feelings,' however, Tom reluctantly had Henrycks look into Craven's activities over the past several weeks.

"Wait, I forgot! There *is* something worth noting!" Justin began. "Doc Craven visited the morgue!"

"Your point, Justin?"

"He could have planted CPU's hair!"

"Is this what you and the ME came up with?" Tom evidently grew impatient.

"The lab was left open unattended for a few minutes on the night Craven visited! The hair was discovered the next day!"

"Where, when and how did he happen to get this hair?" Tom asked.

Tom had him there. He had no clue. It just seemed to be the only reasonable answer based on everything Justin ascertained from Graves and his friend.

"I don't know," Justin admitted sullenly.

Tom let out a loud sigh. "Look, I'm trying to keep an open mind. But evidence is evidence! I have to go where it takes me!"

"I can't change your mind?" Justin asked.

"Get me some evidence!" Tom insisted. "Beverly says you also have good *detective* skills—use *them*!"

****

Justin, Derrick, and CPU had a pizza night at Derrick's. Derrick called pizza "food to calm the anxious heart," which is as close to being poetic as he ever got. But he was right. Justin sat on the floor with his back against the couch. CPU was on the couch and Derrick in a recliner across from the TV—turned on, with the sound off. The aroma of pepperoni, bacon, and cheese prevented anyone from mentioning murders, poisonings, or mayhem.

Derrick could eat a whole pizza. Three pieces satisfied CPU, Justin four. Two large pizzas fit the bill and two liters of soda, plus bread sticks completed the menu. An entire pizza gave way to sleepiness, so Derrick leaned back in the recliner as he tried unsuccessfully to keep his eyes open. CPU cleaned his eyeglasses with a microfiber cloth as he balanced a paper plate containing his first two slices on his lap. He finished cleaning his glasses, adjusted them back on his nose, and noticed the History Channel was beginning a new segment.

Suddenly, CPU called over to Derrick. "Derrick! Turn up the sound!"

Derrick mumbled something.

"Derrick—the sound!" CPU yelled again. He hurled a throw pillow at Derrick's head.

Now alert, Derrick sat up. "*You're* sitting on the remote, Charles!"

CPU searched for the remote, found it stuck in the couch cushion, and increased the TV's volume. Images appeared on the screen with the caption, "Salem Witch Trials: 1692."

From 1692 to 1693, the town of Salem Village, Massachusetts executed two men and several women for the crime of witchcraft. Sixty years later, in 1752, the townspeople incorporated Salem Village and renamed it Danvers. It took decades for families to find restitution for their loved ones who were wrongly convicted. What caught CPU's eye was the new name of the town. By now, Justin and Derrick also made the connection.

"Isn't Danvers where Josiah Krill came from?" Derrick asked.

"Yeah," Justin said. "Hold on a minute."

Justin took out his cell phone containing pictures of all the historical data they had gathered at the library earlier in the week. He grabbed his laptop, opened it up, connected his cell, and downloaded the photos. In a minute the pictures appeared on the larger laptop screen in greater detail making them easier to see. Sure enough, Krill arrived in Angel Falls from Danvers in 1722, shortly after the trials. The artist's drawing of Krill flashed across the screen alongside the newly constructed stone mansion. More textual history appeared and more artist's renderings, until….

"That's where I've seen him! It's the doctor!" CPU yelled. "It's Craven!"

Justin looked closer at the sketch and text beneath it. "The caption says he's Quentin Reese, Krill's butler."

"Well there you go! The butler did it!" Derrick joked.

"I tell you *this* is Doctor Craven!"

"It's gotta be a coincidence—or he's a descendant," Derrick said. "It's a family resemblance—you're not suggesting he's actually three-hundred years old!"

"The state of the bodies, this whole case...we are dealing with the black arts!" CPU insisted. "Krill's household left Danvers to escape the witch trials!"

"That has to be the dumbest thing you've ever said," Derrick said. "There's no such thing as magic or witches!"

"Don't be too hasty, Derrick," Justin interrupted. "The scriptures contain serious warnings against sorcery, necromancy, and witchcraft. If such things didn't exist—or were at least foolish, unholy practices—why would there be warnings against them?"

"And, *have you met Justin*?" CPU asked Derrick. "The supernatural is not unknown to Angel Falls!"

"Of course I've met Justin!" Derrick replied. "What's your point?"

"If Justin does his thing through the power of angels, what makes you think there cannot be an opposing power working through Krill or his butler?" CPU asked.

CPU apparently brought the point home because Derrick suddenly grew quiet.

"Tomorrow we'll pay this doctor a visit," Justin said.

****

A pleasant day arrived for the trio's trip to New Horizons. The sun came out, mixed with soft white cumulus clouds with dark underbellies. The high for the day promised to reach a balmy forty-five degrees. CPU advised everyone during the entire drive of how ill at ease meeting Craven made him feel. Curiosity always laid hold of Derrick, who felt no fear at the moment. Justin's special senses appeared to be on high alert, for reasons he did not understand.

Turning off the main road into New Horizons, Justin headed left for the Medical Center. Finding their way inside the grounds required a small map. CPU already had his copy of the map with him. He used it whenever he worked on residents' computers. He read off directions to Justin. After driving for a mile inside the grounds and executing several turns, they finally pulled into the Medical Center parking lot.

The building looked as large as a small hospital. Craven, Dentists, and other medical specialists ran their practices from here. Some did it on a part-time or on-call basis while others made this their full time practice. Knowing Craven's full-time status, Justin asked to see the doctor at the main desk.

The night before, the boys worked up a pretense for seeing the doctor without making him suspicious. Derrick had the best idea. They would pretend, as journalism students, to be working on a special report. The subject: medical issues peculiar to older Americans. CPU, being the younger of the group, would pose as the student. Derrick and Justin would maintain they came along for moral support.

"That's him—over there!" CPU whispered to Justin. He pointed to a man dressed in standard white lab coat, black pants and shoes, and stethoscope around his neck. But he looked like any other doctor, not a murderer.

They walked over to Craven and Justin reached out to touch his shoulder. All at once, the same malevolent shiver of impending doom ran down his spine. He felt the same awful feeling when he touched the dead body at the morgue. He jerked his hand away quickly, hoping Craven did not notice. Derrick and CPU both noticed but pretended they didn't and said nothing.

Craven turned to face Derrick. "Can I help you?" he asked.

"Maybe you can help my friend here," Derrick nodded toward CPU.

"I'm doing a school paper," CPU said. "Would you have a few minutes for some questions?"

Craven offered to give them just a few minutes of his valuable time, so CPU plied him with a rapid assault of questions. In return, he received information about joint pain, heart problems, forms of dementia and memory issues, problems with weight and blood pressure. All things common to older Americans.

At one point, Derrick chimed in, "Ever get a diagnosis wrong—like thinking headaches were caused by high blood pressure, when there was another cause?"

In his mind Derrick thought, 'like poisoning?'

CPU and Justin gave Derrick a sideways glance. Craven didn't flinch.

Derrick cleared his throat. "I mean, like, do diseases ever get misdiagnosed?"

"Yes, it happens," Craven said. "For example, Lewy Body Dementia, in its early stages, can often be misdiagnosed as Parkinson's."

CPU glanced over at Justin who seemed to signal 'nothing here.' Nothing? It wasn't like Justin to fail at this. He took this as his cue to quit.

"Thanks for your time, Doctor Craven. I should have more than enough information for my report."

"Not a problem, but I do need to get to my patients. You all take care now!" Craven said.

On their way out of the Medical Center, Derrick turned to Justin and asked, "What was with you in there? You looked like you saw a ghost!"

"I noticed it too," CPU said. "Like you got an electric shock when you touched Craven."

"It was a shock," Justin said. "The same thing happened to me at the morgue when I touched one of the victim's bodies."

Derrick's brain went into overdrive, expecting Justin to shoot down his theory, "Maybe Craven's like the living dead or something!"

CPU, always ready to interrupt one of Derrick's stupid ideas, pointed out a familiar-looking car parked at the infirmary.

"It belongs to one of the detectives," Derrick noted.

The moment the words came out of his mouth Justin saw Henrycks leaving the building. "Henrycks is here too," he said. "Looks like he's on the case!"

"Is he following us?" CPU questioned.

"Probably interrogating Craven," Derrick said. "This could be good for you, Chucky!"

"How?" CPU asked. "And do not call me that!"

"He's looking into others besides you," Derrick said, giving CPU a light fist to the shoulder.

"Did you get a look into Craven's eyes?" CPU asked Justin.

"I tried but got sick!" Justin said. "Something's weird about that guy!"

"How weird?" CPU asked. "Like he actually could be Krill's butler weird?"

Justin thought for a moment. "I couldn't get close to him—I don't know why."

"That alone is enough to make *me* suspicious!" Derrick said.

"Did you notice the size of the ring he was wearing?" CPU asked them. "It looked really expensive!"

"It looked old," Derrick said like he couldn't care less. "Kind of ugly too!"

"Rings annoy me, so I don't wear them," Justin said. "Seatbelts everyone!"

"Maybe Derrick's right," CPU said. "We should go back to the library—see if we missed something."

Justin pulled onto the highway and glanced back at CPU. "Like what?"

"The mansion. It has to be hiding secrets," CPU said. "So is everyone who lived in it."

Chapter 10

Henrycks caught up with Tom Selden to update him on his investigation. A fingerprint, found on one of the poisoned pills CPU passed on to the EMT, belonged to Doctor Brent Craven. Based on this new information, Henrycks decided to put a tail on Craven. In the process, he learned some interesting things about Craven's movements. In particular, Craven was making regular trips to the old, abandoned mansion using a very old roadway, which stopped thirty-two yards short of the mansion's main gate.

This old road turned off route 51 further north than Justin and his friends had traveled several days earlier. Had they known about it, they would have saved themselves some walking time. The road appeared to have only recently been cleared, probably within the last month. As the roadway neared the mansion, fallen trees and much heavier undergrowth made further clearing futile without a bulldozer. At that point Craven must have decided to abandon the remaining project. He easily walked the rest of the way to the mansion unencumbered.

Craven's excursions to the mansion only occurred very late at night. Tom agreed; the late-night timing made those trips look suspicious.

"I watched him. He tests the area, looks around like he's checking to see if he's been followed," Henrycks said.

"What could he be up to?" Tom asked, almost rhetorically.

"He brings nothing there and leaves with nothing," Henrycks said. "He's an odd duck, for sure!"

"Does he enter the mansion?"

"Yes. Stays inside an hour or so, then leaves." Henrycks answered.

Neither detective believed in coincidence. Tom agreed with Henrycks' assessment: Craven's interest in the place must not be casual. The doctor's name seemed to pop up frequently. Whatever his connection to current events, he decided the time was right to bring Craven in for questioning. This suited Henrycks, until Tom suggested Justin sit in on the interview.

"Don't you think I can do the job?" Henrycks balked. "Why bring this kid in?"

"The kid's got great intuition, that's why," Tom explained, without giving away Justin's secret. "And he's helped our department before."

****

Jeb Wechsler answered the knock at his cottage door. There stood CPU, grinning on his doorstep. Seeing the young lad standing there surprised Wechsler. CPU, equally surprised, saw Wechsler looking better than he expected.

"You're looking good, Mr. Wechsler!" CPU said.

"Thanks to you, young man! Come on in for a spell." Wechsler said uncharacteristically upbeat.

CPU entered the familiar home; nothing had changed except for its occupant who now, appearing less tense, smiled more than usual. All the old doilies were in place, the plastic still covered the couch. The cottage still smelled like old people. Wechsler led CPU into the kitchen where they sat at the table.

"Have a root beer?" Wechsler asked. CPU accepted. "I got some store-bought cookies too. Have some!" Wechsler plopped a bag of chocolate chips on the table in front of him.

"Thanks," CPU said after a sip of root beer. He grabbed a couple of cookies. "The doctors say you're good now?"

"Better than ever! Can't thank you enough for what you done!" Wechsler said. "No headaches, no shakes, and I sleep like a baby! Can't believe that doctor—I knew he was fishy!"

"First time I was here, you warned me something was wrong. Were you talking about Doctor Craven?" CPU asked.

"All I know is I could see him from my bedroom window those times I couldn't sleep. He'd leave the infirmary in the middle of the night. To top it off, he made my grandson jittery after one of his visits too. Never trusted him!"

"The police are looking for him," CPU said.

"Cops. I see them around a lot, back when I was feelin' sickly," Wechsler said. "Hope they nail the slippery eel to a wall!"

CPU shoved a whole cookie into his mouth and said, "Thef awidy hardanew dogtir?"

"Yeah, we got a new doctor—and don't talk with your mouth full!" Wechsler said. "He seems OK. Came to give me the once over when I was released from the hospital."

"He has to be better than your old doctor!" CPU said with a smile.

CPU washed down the cookie with his remaining root beer. Seeing Wechsler's better-than-usual mood, CPU wondered if Wechsler had heard the sad news yet about his grandson. His new doctor might have been waiting for Wechsler to fully recover before telling him. However, CPU wasn't about to bring up the subject. He just came to check up on Wechsler, who was doing great. Time to leave; but the old man was not quite finished yet.

"Still haven't used the darn laptop since you fixed it!" he told CPU. "But I got this nifty keyboard vacuum. Time to clean off the months of crumbs, dust, and hair what's been collecting on it!"

"Those are nice. Powerful enough to clean but will not suck up any…" CPU stopped, his face frozen in a quizzical expression.

"Any what?" Wechsler asked. When CPU did not answer right away, Wechsler nudged his shoulder. It was like the boy was in a trance.

"What? Uh...Oh! The will not suck up any keys off the keyboard!" CPU finally said. "I need to go!"

CPU jumped up, ran to the living room, and out the front door—but not before he heard Wechsler yell, "Thanks again! And no runnin' through the house!"

"That boy's a tad jittery," Wechsler mumbled as he grabbed a cookie.

****

"Take it easy, Chuck!" Derrick said.

"Don't you see?" CPU urged. "It clears me!"

Justin jumped in. "Charles, I think Detective Selden already realized it. He stopped looking at you a while ago!"

CPU calmed down. "Well, it just makes me feel better knowing how it was done," CPU said.

Detective Selden laid aside the incriminating hair. It would be easy to frame someone with it. He just had no answer for how the kid's hair got placed on the dead boy's body. Henrycks had been a bit slower to accept it. But, with Craven currently in custody, Henrycks also put the matter of the hair to rest for the time being.

"Who'd of thunk it?" Derrick wondered out loud. "Wechsler's hairy laptop keyboard would be the source of the suspicious hair?"

"The question remains: who else had access to it besides Wechsler and possibly the doctor?" Justin asked.

"The police detective," CPU said.

"Even Brian Cosgrove! Wechsler's place was like Grand Central Station—people coming and going!" Derrick said.

"Cosgrove, no. He was a victim!" CPU affirmed. "But, Justin, Detective Selden knew this?"

"Suspected—Selden's good at his job!" Justin said. "Because Craven had access to Wechsler's cottage, your explanation seems likely."

"*If* Craven is the only one who had access," Derrick argued. He looked at his watch then turned to Justin. "Isn't it time for you to do some interrogating?"

Justin glanced at his watch: four forty-five. "I'd better get going! Henrycks is expecting me."

"What if you run into the problem again? What if reading Craven makes you sick?" CPU asked.

"I'll figure it out when I get there," Justin answered.

****

Tom met Justin at the elevator and directed him to Interrogation Room Three. When he got there, Henrycks had already begun questioning Craven, who sat across from him handcuffed to the table. Craven looked confused, but relatively calm under the circumstances. When Henrycks waved Justin in he took the seat next to the detective, facing Craven. It did not take long before Justin began to feel sick.

"You were a hard fellow to track down," Henrycks said to Craven.

"I had no idea anyone was looking for me!" Craven said in protest.

"What's your interest in the old mansion off Route 51?" Henrycks asked.

Craven became irritated. "You've been *following* me?"

"Answer the question," Henrycks shot back. He leaned in closer to his suspect. "And where were you this past few days?"

"I had business in Newburg," Craven answered. He sat back in his chair, straining the cuff's chains. "I own the mansion. I went to Newburg to retrieve the papers."

Justin interrupted with a question of his own. "Are you related to Quentin Reese?"

Craven's face registered complete surprise. "How do you know that?"

Henrycks showed some surprise too. "Yeah, how'd you know? Whose this Reese guy?"

"The original owner's butler," Craven answered. "Krill deeded the place to Reese shortly before everyone vanished. Reese had the deed kept safe in a bank in Newburg. Being the last remaining relative, I had to prove ownership."

"The doctor looks exactly like Reese," Justin said, his head suddenly pounding.

Craven stared pointedly at Justin. "You seem to know an awful lot about me!"

Henrycks threw his arm across Justin as if to shut him up. He asked Craven, "We have another problem, Doc. Why did you try to poison Jeb Wechsler?"

Craven looked at Henrycks like he was crazy. Justin, meanwhile, still could not get a reading off Craven. He felt sicker by the moment. Craven glanced from Henrycks back over at Justin, who understood his expression as a plea for help—help from someone with a degree of sanity. Justin, however, stood up abruptly and left the room. Henrycks brushed it off as nerves and continued questioning Craven.

"Your fingerprints were on pills you prescribed," Henrycks leaned in again, "laced with rat poison and lead! Put Wechsler in the hospital!"

Craven attempted to keep his cool with only partial success. "I have no reason to hurt Mr. Wechsler! I'm his doctor—of course my fingerprints would be on his pills, I prescribed them! I personally handed him his first dose!"

"So you admit to giving him poison?" Henrycks asked.

"Those pills sat on my desk before I delivered them. My office is usually open; anyone could have tampered with them!"

Henrycks' frustration mounted. Craven had an answer for everything! He could hold Craven for seventy-two hours while he looked into his Newburg alibi. But Henrycks wanted more than seventy-two hours. This doctor should be locked away! He should never be allowed to practice medicine again! It was time to see how he handled a murder rap!

As far as he was concerned, Craven was not off the hook concerning Wechsler. Henrycks did not believe in coincidence. Wechsler must have seen something or known something about Craven's other clandestine activities. That knowledge almost got him killed.

Henrycks stood. He paced back and forth, knocking on the table with his fist every few seconds. Craven watched him, worried about what might come next.

"Can I leave?" Craven asked.

Henrycks cleared his throat. "I'm not done with you yet."

Craven fidgeted in his chair. He tested the handcuffs securing him to the table.

"It's no coincidence—you trying to off Wechsler! One of the three murdered boys was related to the old man! He knew what you were up to!"

"I don't know anything about that!" Craven yelled.

"You had means, motive, and opportunity!" Henrycks argued.

"I want a lawyer!"

Henrycks stopped pacing and slammed both hands, palms down, on the table. He stared into Craven's eyes. "You got into the coroner's lab to plant evidence you obtained from Wechsler's laptop to divert attention from yourself."

"Lawyer!" Craven yelled.

******

Justin, sweating and pale, after sitting in on Craven's interrogation, stood outside Tom's office.

Tom motioned to Justin to have a seat. "You don't look so good. What's wrong?" he asked.

Justin took a moment to compose himself, cradling his face in his hands. When he looked up, Tom could see the perspiration around Justin's eyes and mouth.

"Craven makes me sick," Justin said.

"Criminals make me sick too," Tom said in a tongue-in-cheek tone. "But you actually got physically sick from the interview?"

Justin took a deep breath and sat back in the chair. "Any time I try to get inside his head I get ill—I had to leave the room!"

"So you're picking up *something*. Is Craven possessed, a demon?" Tom searched for an answer. "If he has this effect on you isn't something up with him?"

"It would seem so, but I seriously do not know," Justin reluctantly admitted. "But I intend to find out."

Henrycks popped his head into Tom's door. "I'm holding this guy at least until I check his alibi," he said.

"You get much out of him?" Tom asked.

"He's got an answer for everything, but it's all too neat and clean; he's hiding something!"

Henrycks said. "I'm heading to Newburg to check out his story now."

Henrycks drummed on Tom's doorframe a few times then took off. After sitting quietly for another five minutes with Tom, Justin could feel the color return to his face.

"You're looking more yourself," Tom said.

"I'm feeling better, but it's so strange," Justin said. "There was once another person—one with my abilities—who could block me from getting a reading. But Craven is not like me and being blocked never made me sick!"

"Well, maybe Henrycks will pick up on something. In the meantime, I have other cases to work on," Tom said.

Justin took the hint. Time to leave. It was twenty minutes past five, close to dinner time. He would go home, eat dinner, then collect his friends to go back to the library. But his problem with Craven nagged at him. Something he felt, something he could not describe. Perhaps an untapped power inside him tried to tell him something, something he could not yet interpret. A power he did not yet know fully how to use.

He pushed the "down" button at the elevator, stepping inside when the door opened. He hit the ground floor button. As the elevator began its descent, an idea suddenly struck him. He quickly hit the second floor button. The elevator stopped at the second floor, the door opened and Justin cautiously peeked outside.

Here is where prisoners were incarcerated. Guards, officers, and personnel moved about the halls. At the end of one hall was a locked door, beyond the door, jail cells. Before exiting the elevator, Justin concentrated. A mental suggestion to prevent his being seen by anyone echoed up and down the hallway. Slowly, cautiously, he walked toward the locked door. Once at the door, concentrating again, he passed through to the other side.

Looking down at the cells he found only one currently occupied. Doctor Craven sat miserable and alone. Justin walked over to Craven's cell, making sure he was now visible. So far, that sick feeling avoided him. When Craven saw Justin approach he stood and walked to the bars of his cell. Their eyes met, but Justin still felt nothing—no readings, but no illness either.

"You're looking better," Craven said to Justin.

Justin, relieved he did not feel sick, attempted another reading of Craven. Again, nothing. It reminded him of his attempts to read Dawn. He knew Craven did not have the angel gene, so how was he doing this? Being involved in sorcery, as CPU suggested, might explain how he was being blocked. Could a three-hundred-year-old man prevent his powers? None of it made sense. Maybe this guy is just not human.

Justin did not waste any time and came right out with it, "Are you Quentin Reese?"

"Getting right down to business, eh?" Craven said. "Reese died centuries ago!"

"You look just like him," Justin replied. "And you are awfully interested in the mansion off Route 51."

"As I told the detective, I inherited the mansion from my great, great—whatever many 'greats,' grandfather," Craven answered. "My worst crime is *looking* like him!"

Even without a reading, Justin sensed something truthful in this man. But he wished he could be certain. He'd dig further, see if Craven eventually slips up. He asked him about Jeb Wechsler, about the medication that was tampered with. Craven seemed to sense something in Justin too. He answered Justin's questions calmly, in a straightforward manner, as if desperate for someone to believe him.

And Justin did.

One thing became known, Doctor Craven was not in town for at least one of the murders. Anything he knew about the murders he read in the newspaper. There was one other thing, not related to the case, which Justin suddenly remembered. He decided to take advantage of his captive audience to satisfy his own curiosity.

"Are old coins hidden somewhere in the mansion?" Justin asked Craven.

"Honestly, as far as I know, no," Craven said. "I looked around myself—even outside among the grounds. Besides inspecting my property, that's another reason I'd go to the mansion."

"And you found nothing?"

"I found nothing. If Krill wanted granddad to know about some treasure, I'm sure he would have told him."

Another question bugged Justin. Why would Josiah Krill hand over his mansion to his butler? So he asked the doctor, "Krill deeded the mansion to Quentin Reese—why would he do that?"

"It all happened just days before the entire household disappeared," Craven said.

"But why his butler?" Justin asked.

"He was loyal—had been with Krill the longest. A letter he received with the deed explains it all. After the transfer, Reese had all the papers sent to a bank in Newburg for safe keeping."

Justin considered Craven's statement. "It's almost like Krill knew something bad was about to happen."

"He was shrewd. You could be right."

Craven explained he didn't necessarily plan to move into the mansion, although he would leave that option open. His primary thought was to have the local historical society turn it into an historic landmark or museum—possibly even a Bed and Breakfast. But, depending upon how long it took to work out the details, he could end up spending a season or two in the mansion.

"Unfortunately, if I'm arrested, my plans for the mansion may die with me in prison!" Craven admitted.

The area he was in was off limits and Justin completely lost track of time. As fascinating as his stories were, he'd spent enough time talking to Craven. Time to become invisible and make a hasty retreat. Tom Selden needed to know what he just learned, but that would have to wait. He thanked the doctor for the information,, adding he would try to help the doctor get through this. Of course, if Craven was truly innocent as he believed, they were back at square one. No other suspect presented itself!

As Justin headed back down the hallway, Craven called to him. One additional document Craven remembered getting from the bank. In among the deed and other papers was a letter from Krill to Quentin Reece.

"You were right, Krill *must* have had a premonition of impending disaster—he must have been making final arrangements." Craven said. "I say this because in the letter Krill says he suspects a member of the household of some serious impropriety. Only the letter does not go into more detail because Krill only had a strong suspicion. The letter was meant for a warning."

Justin was intrigued. "Doctor Craven, do *you* think whatever upset Krill is what caused everyone to disappear?" he asked.

"Truthfully, yes I do."

Chapter 11

Their second trip to the library did not provide much new information. Derrick suggested skipping ahead several years to see if any new developments about the mansion's disappearance popped up. The lack of such news suggested authorities took a hands-off stance with regard to anything related to the mansion or Josiah Krill. What the news did disclose, the boys already knew: residents of the town were just getting back on their feet after experiencing the worst drought in their history. Consequently, the mansion and its occupants quickly became a distant memory until, finally, it was forgotten altogether.

CPU decided to explore whatever information he could find of Salem during this time. A trip to Massachusetts was out of the question, but here's where the Internet becomes so useful. His computer expertise allowed him to access sites not normally available to the public. It made Derrick and Justin more than a little nervous, but it was not just curiosity driving them. It was imperative they get to the bottom of these murders!

"No wonder Krill was so grouchy!" CPU said. "It says here his wife died of smallpox."

The news surprised Derrick. "He had a wife?"

"Yeah. She died just a year before he started the journey to Grangeville," CPU said.

"Not only that," CPU continued, "he had to sneak her out of Massachusetts—actually brought her here in a coffin!"

"I wonder if she's buried somewhere on the mansion's grounds," Justin said.

"Wouldn't go near her if she was!" Derrick said. "Smallpox...yeech!"

CPU laughed. "After three-hundred years I'm sure she's not contagious!"

"Never mind!" Derrick said. "She's all bones and yeech!"

You could almost see the gears turning in CPU's head. "Maybe Krill wanted to perform some resurrection spell on his wife. He relocated so he would not get caught and burned at the stake!" he said.

"So his wife's the killer?" Derrick asked. "What..."

"Before you poo-poo the idea, do you remember the necromancy books we found in the attic?" CPU asked.

"Now we're getting weird!" Justin said. "Which probably only means we're on the right track, given this is Angel Falls!"

"Maybe Krill had a way to come back. He's the killer!" Derrick said. "But what's his motive for killing?"

"When does a zombie need a motive?" CPU asked. "They feed on the living to survive!"

"Let's check the mansion again—and the grounds," Justin decided. "We'll spend extra time there. We can even look for a grave."

Derrick changed the subject. "Not to change the subject, but do you still believe the doctor is innocent? Without a reading aren't you jumping the gun a little?"

"Yes, Derrick, I do," Justin said. "Uh, I believe he's innocent, not that I'm 'jumping the gun!'"

"Even after everything we've seen—and without a reading?" CPU pressed the point.

"Look, guys, I talked with him. I just had a feeling," Justin admitted. "You know, I relied on good old human intuition."

Derrick made the raspberry sound with his lips. "You need a tune-up!"

"Why I didn't get sick this last time—I don't know! Let's just leave it at that!" Justin said.

****

Detective Henrycks tore into Tom's office, infuriated. "He's missing—escaped!" he yelled.

Tom Selden always kept his cool but looked a bit miffed by this alarming intrusion into his office. "Who escaped?"

"Craven! He's not in his cell!"

"Can't be!" Tom jumped out of his chair, ran past Henrycks, and out of his office. "C'mon, let's go!"

Hitting the elevator, they got off on the second floor. Tom nearly ran into the officer guarding the jail cells at the end of the hall. Henrycks trailed close behind. He ordered the officer to let them in to inspect a prisoner. When they got to Craven's cell it was empty—locked shut, but empty. Tom immediately went back to the officer to question him.

"Rivers, has anyone been down here in the last two hours?" Tom asked the startled and confused officer.

"Edwards transported a prisoner into cell nine about an hour ago," Officer Rivers said.

"And you've been here the whole time?"

"Since three o'clock today, sir!" Rivers said.

"Henrycks, go see what Edwards has to say and get back to me, OK?" Tom ordered.

"You got it!" Henrycks replied. He turned and went back toward the elevator.

"Sir?" Rivers interrupted. "I did see a young boy down here earlier, by the elevator. Only he was getting into the elevator to leave; he was not down this way."

"Describe him," Tom ordered.

"Teenage, about six-two, sandy haired. Had on a green, hooded coat," Rivers said.

"Justin! Did he say anything to you?"

"Never came down here, like I said. Didn't hear him say nothing to no one at the elevator either."

"Rivers, think! Did you ever see him get *off* the elevator?"

"No, sir. Just getting on."

"OK, thanks Rivers! Carry on!"

Tom took the elevator back to the third floor and went to his office to think. He shut the door behind him and slumped into his chair. Questions flooded his brain. It had to be Justin. What was he doing down there? Curious. How could he only be seen getting on the elevator when no one saw him get off in the first place?

A horrible thought crossed Tom's mind. Did Justin have something to do with Craven's escape? A sudden knock at his door interrupted his thoughts. It was Detective Henrycks.

Tom motioned him to enter.

"Edwards says Craven was in his cell at 5:10 today when he delivered his prisoner," Henrycks said. "He left only ten minutes later to go home—where he is currently."

"Have you seen Justin?" Tom asked.

"Not since the interrogation," Henrycks said. "He got sick and left."

"Yeah, he came to see me for a few minutes then decided to go home."

"When was that?" Henrycks asked.

Tom suddenly looked dismayed. "Right about the time Craven went missing."

"You're not thinking…" Henrycks began.

Tom shot Henrycks an exasperated look. "I'm certainly going to look into it!"

****

With the events of the day before, Tom did not sleep well. Today he rushed through his morning routine as soon as he got up. Once at the office, he impatiently sat through two meetings, interviewed a prospective patrol officer, then finished up some overdue paperwork. With those items out to the way, before he did anything else, Tom gave Beverly a call. When he discovered she was out to lunch at her favorite diner, he decided a face-to-face would be better. He trusted Beverly more than anyone else in Angel Falls—or anywhere else on planet Earth for that matter. She also knew Justin better than he did.

Before he grilled Justin on his whereabouts he'd get her insights on the young man.

The diner Beverly often frequented was within walking distance of the Tribune. Tom found her seated in a booth by a window. Just as her lunch order arrived, he approached her booth. Surprised to see him standing there, Beverly invited him to sit across from her and join her for lunch. In the midst of all his rushing around this morning, Tom didn't realize just how hungry he was; he had forgotten to eat breakfast, so he joined her.

He ordered what she was having, a Reuben with fries and an iced tea. Talking to Beverly was always easy, but knowing the strength of her friendship with Justin, he entered into the conversation with caution. Beverly knew Craven had been imprisoned. It was her job to know the goings-on in Angel Falls. She ate her Reuben as Tom described the previous day's events. When he got around to the moment when Justin left his office, she questioned where Tom was going with this information. Then he got to the point.

"Craven escaped from jail yesterday evening," Tom said, swallowing hard. He put his Reuben back on the plate to take a sip of iced tea.

Beverly's mouthful of iced tea shot across the booth, onto Tom's shirt. "Tom, no! How?"

"Looking into it," Tom said. He grabbed a napkin to wiped tea off his shirt. "I need to ask you something."

"Me? What?"

Tom cleared his throat and began, "Would Justin ever use his 'gifts' to break out a prisoner?"

Beverly leaned forward, narrowing her eyes, "Is that what this is about?"

"It's like the guy disappeared—like a magician!" Tom explained. "Nobody saw anything! There's only one person I know of who could perform such a feat!"

"Why do you think Justin agreed to let you in on his secret? He respects you, the law, and wants to remain accountable!"

"Sorry, Bev. I had to ask."

"Well, the answer is emphatically, *No*! He wouldn't do that kind of 'trick' as you call it!"

"I still need to talk to him. Maybe he can tell me who could do this. Any idea where I can find him?"

Beverly finished her lunch, wiped her mouth with a napkin, and dropped it on the table. She stood, turned to go pay her bill, but momentarily looked back at Tom. "He's on assignment. Check the Botanical Gardens. Once he's done there, it's anybody's guess. You're the detective, go find him yourself!"

Chapter 12

Fletcher Byrd peered carefully up and down the street. There was no moon; dark rolling clouds filled the night sky. The meadow across from him lay silent in deep shadows. Not even a cricket could be heard. Sleep occupied the few houses along this stretch of road. All was quiet—dark and quiet, as Fletcher liked it. Hot wiring most cars came easy for Fletcher, but this one numbskull left the keys in the ignition. It was as if the owner thought nobody ever would ever come to this isolated place. Perhaps the car's deplorable condition served as a built-in security system! Fletcher liked much newer models, but this one would do. It's the ride that mattered— and avoiding the cops.

Fletcher yanked open the unlocked driver-side door and hopped in. The old Mazda started up, slowly pulling away from the curb, headlights off for the moment. Once he made it to the end of the street, the lights came on, the engine revved up, and Fletcher was on his way.

After five minutes, Fletcher pulled into a Sunoco MiniMart. Grabbing some Doritos, and a two-liter bottle of Mountain Dew, he moved to the back of the store. From there he called out to the lone night shift employee at the front of the store.

"Hey, you got a leak or something back here!" Fletcher called.

The employee left the register to head back where Fletcher was, "Hold on! Show me!"

As the employee made his way to the back, Fletcher stooped low behind the racks of products to remain unseen. He hurriedly moved to the front of the store. Before bolting out the door he reached for a pack of cigarettes from behind the register. Seconds later, outside in the car, he started her up. Tires screeching across the parking lot, he raced to the exit, but stopped suddenly. The car entering the parking lot looked like an unmarked cop car. Fletcher slowed to approach the exit more cautiously. The cop, entering the lot, casually glanced over at him. Fletcher breathed a sigh of relief as the cop passed him by and pulled into a parking space. Fletcher stepped on the gas and peeled out onto the road, glancing back quickly to see the cop enter the mart.

Going for the open road, he hit Route 51 and headed north as snow began to fall. He opened up the Mazda blasting past several vehicles until he thought better of it. Too late. The lights of a hidden patrol car suddenly lit up behind him. Fletcher went into preservation mode. He turned off the car's headlights. Quickly rounding a curve in the highway, at a point out of sight of the cop, he did a sudden U-turn, quickly pulling off into tall grass on the other side of the road.

Hidden in the tall grass, Fletcher shut the engine and waited. As expected, the cop flew past his location. Must have been doing seventy-five, lights flashing, siren blaring. It wasn't the first time Fletcher gave them the slip. Now seemed like a good time to end this joy ride and leave the car where it was. He wiped the steering wheel, keys and anything else he touched then exited the car. Being careful to remain hidden from the main road, Fletcher exited the car and headed further into the woods.

Getting scratched by thorns and slowed down by heavy weeds got annoying until Fletcher finally stumbled upon a cleared pathway. Movement was easier, but before long, this new path now became blocked by trees and dense undergrowth. Cursing his luck, Fletcher looked around for a better escape route. It was very dark, but suddenly something became visible through the trees. A bright blue light beat on and off one hundred yards ahead. His head throbbed the longer he stared at it. Its eerie pulsing rhythm beat in unison with his heart.

Fletcher momentarily regained his senses as his eyes adjusted to his surroundings. There, just beyond the trees stood a broken down stone building. The blue glow emanated from that building! Fletcher felt chilled. Along with the snow, the temperature continued to fall. The house looked warm, inviting him to find shelter from the cold. He managed to take a step toward the house when a sudden, sharp pain to the back of his head made everything go black.

Fletcher woke to find himself flat on his back in a musty smelling room with no lights except for the pulsing blue. A severe headache prevented him from looking around. Over his head he was barely able to make out the shadowy image of a bird, maybe an owl. It just hung there motionless, staring back at him. Sitting up sickened him. The room's odor intensified the nausea. He managed to sit, to lean forward and rest his head between his knees. This felt better if he sat very still. After a several minutes he was able to raise his head where a large mirror loomed directly over him—the source of the radiating a blue light!

Fletcher felt a presence, a movement in the shadows. "Whose there?"

His heart continued to pound in unison with each wave of blue light. Beads of sweat formed on his forehead. Something *did* move in the shadows! Taking a deep breath to steady himself, Fletcher slowly stood up, lurched forward, staggering, but managed to keep from falling over.

A low, subdued voice came from the shadows, "It will be over soon."

"Who are you?" Fletcher yelled. "What do you want?"

An attempt to look around made him nauseous. Throbbing blueness filled his aching head and distorted his vision, his heart controlled by its rhythm.

"What do I want? Your life force, of course!" the voice mocked.

The blue intensified, its rhythm increased. Fletcher stood, transfixed when snakelike, the flash struck. It grabbed Fletcher, engulfing him in its death grip. Immediately, skin on his face and chest tightened. Pain seared through his entire body. He screamed, but the sound choked inside his closing throat. His eyeballs shrank and fell back inside his skull. The bones in his legs snapped under his weight, bringing him crashing to the floor. With a final wrenching, twisting sensation of his backbone he was gone. The blue light retreated back inside the mirror and was gone.

****

Tom Selden leaned over his desk and stared down at Justin. He was fuming! "The prisoner area is strictly off limits to civilians!" he shouted. "You had no business being down there!"

Justin squirmed uncomfortably in his chair. He tried to think. "I should have come to you first," was all he could say.

"What possessed you to go in the first place?"

"To see if my hunch was correct," Justin said. "I wanted to see if I could get close to Craven, one on one—get a reading without getting sick."

"So, what happened?" Tom asked, his demeanor calming some.

"Nothing—that's the thing! I didn't get sick, but I still couldn't get inside his head!"

Tom let out a deep sigh. He took his seat, elbows on desk, hands folded together. "Look, Justin, work with me. Don't go all Lone Ranger on me. Bev says it's the reason why you came to me. I could certainly use your help but pull stuff like this and we'd all get into trouble!"

"I'm sorry. I wasn't thinking! I promise, no more clandestine actions on my part!"

Suddenly, Tom's phone rang. He picked it up. As he listened to the person on the other end, his face paled. When the conversation ended he gently replaced the handset back onto the receiver.

"More trouble," Tom said somberly. "Another body—just like the others—has been found. With Craven on the loose again, it really looks bad for him!"

"My gut tells me he's being framed," Justin said.

"Framed? Isn't that a bit of a stretch, Justin! Why do you insist he's innocent? Do you have any—uh, what's it called—*Proof*?"

"Without a reading, no."

"Do some detective work, get your forces back on track!" Tom urged. "The doctor goes missing, we suddenly have another death. This is too much of a coincidence to be ignored—and I don't like coincidences!"

Justin steeled himself. "You're right, that's what I plan to do. Do some detecting and get to the bottom of this!"

Tom half smiled in spite of himself. "Just remember what I told you about being a Lone Ranger!"

Justin got up to head home—for real this time—when Tom stopped him. He handed Justin an envelope. "Put this on Detective Henrycks' desk on your way out, will you?" he asked.

Justin took the envelope and headed down the hall. Henrycks was not at his desk, which held a neatly stacked pile of papers. There was also a folder containing information on Doctor Craven. It seemed odd neither Henrycks nor Tom had any family photos on their desks. But, with neither being married, what photos would they display? Justin continued, out of curiosity, to study items on Henrycks' desk, until he heard the detective's voice approaching.

Justin did not want to engage in a second scolding from this detective. He hurriedly dropped the envelope onto the desk and shot out of Henryck's office toward the elevator. He was in luck. At that opportune moment, the elevator door opened. He ducked inside the elevator just as Henrycks came into view. With a push of the button for the parking garage, the doors shut and Justin headed for home.

****

Brent Craven had no idea where he was or how he got there. The room was dark. Only a small amount of dim light entered through a hole in the ceiling where a large tree limb had broken through. He was on the floor, his wrists tied to a bed with zip ties. His feet, stretched out in front of him, were also zip tied around his ankles. The windows were covered with heavy, old drapes. A musty odor filled the damp room. His wrists were bloodied and sore from attempts to break free.

He heard movement outside the door to the room, but no voices or other sounds. Eventually, even the movements ceased leaving him completely alone in deathly silence. How long he had been imprisoned he did not know, but his stomach and dry mouth made it clear it was at least the good part of a day. The throbbing he felt in his head earlier finally diminished a bit. Being exhausted, Doctor Craven relented in his struggle and rested. Certainly someone would notice he was missing and come look for him.

****

The front page of next day's newspaper included a school photo of the newest victim of the Angel Falls serial killer. Fletcher Byrd's identity, including his personal history and police record, appeared alongside the photo. Learning of yet another victim motivated Justin and company more than ever to solve these crimes and prevent further deaths. However, CPU's fear level rose along with his level of motivation. Most of the victims were close to his age. Because of failing grades Fletcher Byrd, although a year older, had been in CPU's class.

How the killer moved about unseen remained a mystery. Not one witness could be found to come forward with information that would help solve the case. Derrick no longer considered the culprit to be an extraterrestrial. Now it had to be a vampire: goes unseen, kills at night, completely drains his victims!

Why the killer went after the younger set, not older adults, also remained a mystery. CPU thought the killer would be someone much older, even frail or handicapped. He therefore found it easier to attack kids. Justin reminded CPU that all his victims were strong, healthy, individuals. They would easily have fought off such an attacker.

Justin was formulating is own ideas which is why he liked CPU's idea of giving the mansion another look. The old ruin had become the center of attention of late. Justin guessed someone else must have an interest in it too, not just Craven. Derrick suggested the vampire needed a place to store his coffin. A spooky old house fit the bill. While not disputing a possible supernatural aspect to the case, both Justin and CPU strongly dissuaded him from his vampire theory. None of the bodies had a mark on them, no puncture wounds, cuts or bite marks of any kind!

The ride to the mansion went quickly. It was a nice, sunny day in the forties—just a tad warmer than usual for this time of year. Thanksgiving was just around the corner—something the boys had almost forgotten about for obvious reasons. They turned off onto the old dirt road and continued on it as far as they could go. Entering through the same window they used last time, they moved slowly, but deliberately, toward the stairway, investigating every square inch along the way. Each of them carried a flashlight filled with new batteries.

Derrick's excitement rose when, again, he found a 1796 half dime sticking out from under the baseboard in the living room. With elevated expectations, he concentrated his light along the remaining baseboards.

"The man upstairs might get angry if you take his money," CPU warned.

Derrick, pausing his search momentarily, looked at CPU quizzically. "Who, God?"

"No, Krill—he's at the top of the stairs watching you!" CPU joked.

Derrick poo-pooed CPU's comment and continued to search for more old money. Justin insisted he stop hunting for coins so they could all head upstairs. When the three reached the landing at the top of the stairs CPU looked up at the portrait of Josiah Krill, pointed toward Derrick, and said, "Better check his pockets!"

Derrick gave him a shove down the hall.

"OK guys, knock it off. We're here to find evidence!" Justin urged.

Each room was more carefully searched this time. Nothing glaring stood out. Except, when they hit the third room on the left, Derrick spotted something next to the bed.

"What is it?" CPU asked.

"Don't touch it, Charles!" Derrick warned. "It could be evidence. I've used these to strap down car batteries. It's part of a zip tie."

"Also used as restraints," Justin added. "Someone's been here."

Justin pulled a plastic, sealable sandwich baggie from his back pocket. He brought several along in case they actually found some worthwhile evidence. He also brought a pair of tweezers along, which he used to pick up the item Derrick found. With the evidence securely placed inside the baggie, Justin sealed it up and placed it back into his pocket.

"Neat!" CPU said. "You came prepared!"

"Let's finish checking the rest of the house," Justin said.

The remaining rooms held nothing of interest. Finally, at the end of the hall, they faced the familiar attic doorway. The door was open; all was quiet at the top of the stairs.

"We're not going up there, are we?" CPU asked, hoping for a 'no' answer.

Just then, Justin noticed something partially hidden by the door. Closing the door revealed a pack of cigarettes on the floor. Reaching into his pocket he pulled out another Ziplock baggie, carefully placing the pack of cigarettes inside.

"More evidence?" CPU asked.

"Fletcher smoked, didn't he?" Justin asked. Both Derrick and CPU nodded 'yes' in agreement.

"This off-brand is only sold in one place—the MiniMart not far from here," Derrick said.

With the mention of the MiniMart something clicked in Justin's head. He smiled broadly. Tom wanted proof, this could be it! Something finally began to make sense now! If only he could trace the movements of Fletcher just before he died. That information could lead them to the killer!

"No need to go any further," Justin said. "Let's get out of here."

CPU breathed a sigh of relief.

"What's on your mind?" Derrick asked. "You're not saying cigarettes killed Fletcher?"

"Maybe," Justin said, "indirectly!"

Chapter 13

A pleasant surprise met Beverly this particular morning. She had not seen Justin for several days, yet there he stood waiting for her outside her office. After motioning for him to enter they exchanged some small talk and caught up on events in their personal lives. However, Justin seemed eager to get onto a different subject. He pulled two sealed sandwich baggies from his coat pocket, gently laying them on her desk.

She picked up one of the bags and asked, "What are these?"

"Evidence," Justin answered. "I need you to do something for me—give them to Tom."

"Why don't you?" She asked.

"He'll have a barrage of questions I'm not ready to answer—not yet."

"What do you want *me* to tell him?" She asked.

"To get fingerprints off them. I need to confirm something before I go accusing anyone."

Beverly looked surprised. "You mean the serial killer?"

"Yes. Tom wanted proof and I'm about to get it. This is part of it, but I still have one more thing to do."

"You finally got to go inside Craven's head?"

"No. And it's not him," Justin said.

"Didn't all the evidence point to the doctor?" Beverly asked.

"Evidence was manipulated to make it look like the doctor," Justin explained.

"So where is the doctor now? Right after he escaped from jail another body was found!"

"I don't know, but someone is getting desperate," Justin said. "There have been several attempts by someone to focus the blame on others."

"Like CPU, or that Jeb Wechsler resident at New Horizons?"

"Exactly!"

Beverly examined Justin as he sat across from her. She suddenly realized he reached his conclusions without using his angelic abilities.

"You haven't lost your powers, have you?" she asked. "Using your 'gut' like a regular detective, not a superhero!"

"If I'm right, I'll still need to use them," Justin replied. "But only when the time is right. I'll need to get Tom involved too."

"You be careful," Beverly said.

****

At Justin's request, Derrick cut out Fletcher's photo from the newspaper. After collecting CPU, the three of them drove out to the MiniMart together. With any luck the same evening-shift clerk would be on duty. The necessity for this particular excursion mystified Derrick and CPU. Justin continued to maintain a closed-mouthed attitude about it. The Honda pulled up to the Mart, parked and the three went inside.

Justin motioned to Derrick for the newspaper photo. No one else was in the MiniMart at the time, except for the clerk behind the register.

Justin approached him, "Were you here last Tuesday night?"

The clerk took a moment to think about it and finally said, "Yeah, I was here. Why?"

Justin showed him the photo. "Was this guy in here that night?"

The clerk recognized the kid in the photo immediately. "He ran out without payin'!"

"So he was here?" Justin asked again.

"Sure! Did the cops get him?"

"You put out a 9-1-1 call?" Justin asked.

"No. A cop was here soon after the kid vamoosed. He bought a few things then went after him," the clerk said.

"Describe the cop."

Pointing to Derrick the clerk said, "Husky like him—only bald."

Derrick and CPU gaped at each other, hit by the sudden realization who the cop was. Justin, however, did not seem at all phased, but pleased! He thanked the clerk for the information. As the three were about to exit the Mart, the clerk called to Justin.

"Did the cops catch the guy? I ain't heard nothin'."

"Yeah, he got caught," Justin called back.

****

The caller ID on Beverly's office phone said "Tom Selden." She smiled, picked up the call, and greeted her friend. It had been two days since she dropped off Justin's items for forensics to examine. Tom had some news, and some questions which Beverly did not have answers to. She did not know where Justin found the items. He never explained what he hoped forensics would find. He only said the items contained the proof Tom was looking for.

Tom wondered what Justin was thinking sending him these items as evidence. Evidence of what? One of the items, the zip tie, had Detective Henrycks' fingerprints on it. These were standard issue for detectives. Where did Justin find them? The other item, the cigarettes, were covered in Fletcher

Byrd's prints. Tom could see no obvious use for this information—they belonged to the victim.

This call grew more disappointing as Tom droned on about his issues with Justin. She especially felt bad about the tension that erupted between her two friends at police headquarters. She could understand Tom's position, some areas of headquarters are off limits for good reason. But, because of Justin's exceptional nature, she hoped Tom would overlook this youthful indiscretion. The boy had a zealous spirit, sincere and wholehearted. She tried to convince him Justin's exuberance did not excuse his actions, but he meant well. He was bound to make mistakes, but she assured Tom he would tow the line in the future.

By Tom's change in tone over the phone, Beverly felt he had begun to acquiesce. She made some progress. Relieved, she let him know Justin's current whereabouts, as far as she knew them. Based on what Justin confided in her earlier, she assured Tom he would soon have some answers.

"He's following a hunch," she told him. "He'll want to talk to you about it."

"I wish he'd come to me first," Tom said. "But I guess I can't fault him for going to you first—especially after the lecture I gave him."

"I can tell you this much," Beverly continued, "He insists on Doctor Craven's innocence—says evidence against him is fabricated."

"Interesting you should mention it, Bev," Tom said. "There was a very small piece of additional evidence our forensics team noticed, on the zip tie. It was almost missed."

"What?" Beverly asked.

"A tiny spec of blood and skin. We got the DNA results."

"Whose blood?" Beverly asked.

"Doctor Craven's."

****

As they left the MiniMart parking lot, Derrick realized he misplaced his cell phone.

"Did you have it at my house?" Justin asked.

"I don't think so; I don't know!" Derrick said.

"I don't think you did," CPU stated. "I remember thinking it's not in your back pocket where you usually keep it."

"Why didn't you say something?" Derrick thought a moment, trying to retrace his steps. He asked Justin, "Can we go back to the mansion—It must have dropped out of my pocket when we were inside."

Justin laughed, CPU groaned at the thought of returning to that freakish place.

"Sorry guys!" Derrick said.

They drove back out to route 51 and pulled into the same dirt road they had earlier the day before. About three-hundred-feet into the woods CPU noticed something shiny off to their left. When he called out, Derrick noticed it too and urged Justin to stop the car. The three got out to investigate. It turned out to be a car—an old Mazda! The Mazda was well hidden from the main road. Inside, on the front seat, Justin noticed an open bag of Doritos plus a half-finished, two-liter bottle of Mountain Dew.

"Looks like the driver went to the MiniMart," Justin remarked. "Derrick, can you take down the license plate?"

Derrick took out a pad and pen, which he often kept handy, to write down the plate. He tore off the page and gave it to Justin.

CPU spoke up about reading something about a stolen car. Buried deep inside the Tribune, the theft occurred the same night the MiniMart was robbed. CPU reasoned that Fletcher must have graduated from petty theft to grand theft auto. The paper did not reveal the owner or mention if the car had been found yet. A short-lived police chase on Route 51 resulting in the disappearance of the perpetrator summed up the news report.

They took the rest of the way to the house on foot. Justin's tight-mouthed silence had Derrick and

CPU whispering along the way, trying to guess what their mission was. Had Justin changed his mind? Did he now suspect Craven was the serial killer? Did Henrycks, upon catching Craven in the act, arrested him at the mansion, although not in time to save Fletcher?

Once they worked their way inside the mansion, CPU called Derrick's phone. They listened intently for his ring tone, the theme to the once popular TV show 'Castle.' Derrick hated to see the show end. Finding a downloadable ring tone of the show's theme eased his sense of loss. They heard nothing, so they decided to move further inside the house and try again. This time, very faintly, they heard it. It was coming from the second floor.

CPU ended the call as the three of them trekked up the stairs, past old Krill's now familiar portrait, and into the hallway.

"I thought I saw Mr. Krill smile as we came up the stairs," CPU said.

"Funny," Derrick replied in a deadpan monotone to let CPU know it wasn't.

CPU pressed redial once more. Much louder this time, the sound came from the other end of the hallway. Once there CPU tried again. The phone was in the attic!

Derrick became troubled. "It can't be," he said. "We didn't go up to the attic last time!"

"But there it is," Justin said. "Your phone is up there!"

"Krill took your phone because you took his half-dime," CPU goaded him.

"Do we really need to go up there?" Derrick said, ignoring his younger friend.

"You want your phone, don't you?" Justin asked.

Reluctantly, Derrick started up the stairs. Justin and CPU followed. Halfway up something hit them, stopping them dead in their tracks. A savage roar like a violent windstorm waylaid their ears and brought shivers up and down their spines.

Derrick covered his ears, as did the others, and shouted, "Forget the phone! I'm due for an upgrade anyway!"

****

Beverly's phone conversation with Tom did not go as well as she hoped. The evidence Justin passed along to Beverly failed to convince Tom. It could just as easily be interpreted that Henrycks captured Craven, who subsequently got away after killing Fletcher. He told Beverly as much. Finding a pack of cigarettes in the old house only proved Fletcher was there, not where he was killed. His body was found near Falls High School like the others, without a shred of additional evidence.

"I have to disagree, Tom," she said, cradling the phone receiver against her shoulder. "At least give his theory some consideration. I've seen him work. He's a natural detective, his special abilities notwithstanding!"

"And I didn't get my badge in a cereal box!" Tom balked.

"Sorry, Tom! I didn't mean…"

Tom cut her off. "Never mind, Bev. His recent shenanigans tell me his level of maturity, both as a person and detective, is not up to par."

"So you're going to cut him off? Ignore him completely?"

"When he comes up with something that makes real sense, I might listen. Until then, and like I've told him, I go with the evidence!"

"I didn't mean to insult you—sorry!"

"And Beverly, I'm still skeptical. From all I've seen so far, a magician like David Copperfield could do the same trick Justin did in my office!"

Tom's admission took Beverly by surprise. Plus, he never called her by her full name unless he was upset with her. He could be so exasperating! Well, two can play at that game!

"Thomas, you know me better—I, we, didn't pull a fast one on you! How can you say that? How can you deny what we both saw?"

"Just sayin'," came his terse reply before hanging up the phone.

****

Doctor Craven's restored consciousness came accompanied by an aching head with the lingering odor of chloroform. He sensed he had been moved to a new location. Instead of a bed, he was now sitting, tied to a chair. The room was darker than the last location. As far as he was able to discern, there were no windows. As his head slowly cleared he sensed a presence lurking nearby. Something moved.

"Who's there?" Craven called into the darkness.

More rustling from his right. Then the clearing of a throat.

"How did you get here," a Voice asked. "if you say there is no treasure!"

Craven struggled with the zip ties. They cut into his wrists. His feet, tied together to one leg of the chair, did not budge. "Are you crazy—what is this about?" Craven yelled into the darkness.

"The most likely place *would* be the mausoleum," the Voice, calm and low, said. "I am surprised I missed this!"

"Who are you?" Craven insisted.

"You've forgotten your old friend, Quentin?" the Voice asked. "You must be here for a reason; you must know its whereabouts!"

Craven struggled again against his restraints. "Where's what—*what* are you babbling about?"

"Krill's treasure, of course!" the Voice answered. "Or should I say *my* treasure!"

An incredible thought struck Craven. *This madman thinks he's his ancestor, Quentin Reese! First it was that tall kid, Justin, asking the same thing!* If he could only see this guy's face it might tell him something about him. Craven heard stories of a fortune in priceless artifacts Krill supposedly tucked away somewhere before he disappeared. Just stories, for sure, but Craven decided to play along to find out more about his captor.

"How do you know about the treasure?" Craven asked.

The Voice returned with another question. "How did you escape the mirror?

"What mirror?"

A long, wooden object, maybe a cane, jabbed Craven sharply in the ribs. "I grow tired of this; tell me where to find the treasure, Quentin!"

Angered, Craven shot back, "Firstly, you lunatic, I'm Doctor Brent Craven, not Quentin Reese! Secondly, stop answering my questions with a question! Finally, there is no treasure!"

Several moments of sudden silence elapsed until Craven spoke up again. "I am the only living descendant of Mr. Reese, who died hundreds of years ago! I own the mansion, and there never was a treasure!"

"You look very much like him!" the Voice said after a moment. "But, perhaps you speak the truth!"

"How do you know about Krill and Reese?" Craven shouted. "What's your interest in the estate?"

A loud, menacing laugh pierced the room. "It's not important, *Craven*. What the police believe you to be guilty of *is* important however!"

"They released me due to a lack of evidence!"

"I plan to change their minds, doctor!" the voice retorted.

Nervous confusion suddenly filled Craven. What could have happened between his release from jail and his abduction by this psycho? What could he possibly know?

"People will be looking for me if I don't return to work soon!" Craven told his captor.

The Voice laughed again. "They are already looking for you, sir! My plan is to remove you permanently from society. Then I will stake my claim to the mansion; it's fool-proof!"

"You won't get away with this!" Craven shouted. "My reputation speaks for itself, you demented putz!"

Another loud burst of maniacal laughter from his captor brought knots to Craven's stomach. Then came a moment of eerie silence before the shadow voice had one final thing to say.

"You will remain here until I am ready to release you! I, on the other hand, have more to do."

Craven heard some movement, a low grinding sound, then complete silence again. As sweat rolled down his forehead he wondered what the faceless voice still needed to do. Whatever it was, he feared the time he had left in this world would soon be gone!

Chapter 14

The roar from the attic continued even louder.

"C'mon, Let's get out of here!" Derrick insisted above the noise. "I really am due for an upgrade!"

Justin shouted over the roar. "What about your pictures, your apps?"

"Forget about them!"

CPU, with his eyes closed, called out, "He can re-download everything onto a new phone!"

"I don't care! I have to see what's going on up there," Justin argued.

He sprinted up the remaining stairs to the attic two steps at a time. Derrick and CPU, more ready to run back down the stairs, watched in astonishment instead. The moment Justin reached the attic, the windstorm ceased as abruptly as it began. An odd, fluorescent-like glow illuminated the floor, which allowed Justin to find the phone. It lay on the floor about six feet in front of the mirror. Justin looked around the attic for the source of the light. It seemed to come from the boxes behind him, but then he realized the source was the mirror itself!

"Hey, guys—come look at this!" he called to his friends.

"What for?" they yelled in unison.

"C'mon, everything's quiet now!" Justin said. "You have to see this!"

Reluctantly, Derrick and CPU made their way slowly up the stairs and made their way beside Justin, in front of the mirror.

"Do you see it?" Justin asked. "The light is coming from *inside* this mirror!"

"Maybe there's LEDs built into it?" Derrick supposed out loud.

"The mirror is way too old, like the rest of this house!" CPU corrected. "LED technology did not exist back then."

"Duh! Thanks, Mr. Science!" Derrick, coming around to his old self, sneered.

Justin handed Derrick his phone, who pocketed it. All of a sudden the storm sound returned. Looking into the mirror, they saw a dark, swirling cloud-like thing materialize. All three boys reacted in unison, quickly turning to look behind them. They expected to see the cloud expanding in front of the boxes stacked by the back wall. There was nothing there. When they looked back at the mirror the cloud had grown larger. They took another quick look behind them. Still nothing!

"*That* thing's coming from *inside* the mirror too!" CPU yelped. "It's like what I saw the first time we were here—it's no raccoon, Derrick!"

"CPU, uh, contractions!" Derrick muttered, horrified at the twisting cloud.

The boys stood transfixed. The cloud billowed and contracted, moving ever closer to the front of the mirror. As the shape shifted and twisted, the undulating sound rose and fell. Slowly, a form took shape at the top of the cloud. It flattened then rounded. Two hollow openings took form until two eyes stared out at them. Details of a face, grave and stoney, solidified. The mouth moved, contorted in a fearful expression. The sound died down.

"Leave this place!" the face, without sound, appeared to warn.

"It's Josiah Krill!" CPU choked out the words.

"Wha...What's he say... saying?" Derrick barely whispered.

"There is only death here!" Krill mouthed more strenuously.

Justin took one step forward. Then a second step, to look into the eyes of the image in the mirror. An instantaneous, powerful connection knocked him off balance sending him backwards onto the floor. In an instant he knew the anguish of Josiah Krill. Imprisoned more than three hundred years, he had lost all hope. The impact of their connection visibly affected Krill too, as his entire image momentarily dispersed in a flurry of atoms, then reassembled. Upon its reassembly, Krill's features had changed, actually softened slightly.

"What do you want?" Justin asked the image of Krill.

"Stop him!" the image mouthed.

Derrick leaned in just a little closer, his ears strained to hear the voice. "You can hear him?" he asked Justin.

"I've developed a connection, so yes."

"What *does* he want?" CPU asked.

"Shhh! Let me listen…. Stop who?" Justin asked.

"Whom," CPU corrected.

Krill's mouth convulsed the answer, "Yakob steals the life force to survive!"

"We don't know a Yakob! Where do I find him?" Justin asked.

Krill's image managed one last word, "The mirror…." then it suddenly trembled, ebbed, and dispersed, leaving the boys to stare at themselves in the mirror.

****

Excited chattering filled the Honda on the drive back to Justin's. Derrick and CPU bombarded

Justin with questions about Krill. What was he like? What did he want? Why or how did he get inside a mirror? Who was Yakob? Justin's connection with Krill at the mansion revealed one important bit of information: sorcery played a major role in the disappearance of Krill's household, and now, these murders! Alex, Brian, and Fletcher all had their 'Life Force' absorbed by this Yakob character!

Further down the road the chattering died down. Derrick, sitting shotgun as usual, stared out the window as Justin drove. CPU checked his phone.

In an outburst of excitement, CPU suddenly shrieked, "Yakob!"

Derrick, startled, jumped in his seat and hit his head. "Ow—C'mon! You gotta stop doing that Charles!"

"I know who Yakob is—I read about him!"

"Well goodie for you! Next time let us know with your 'inside' voice!" Derrick ordered, rubbing his ears and the top of his head.

"I remember reading about a Yakob Heimrich at the library! I have it here on my phone. I will bet this is who Krill was talking about!" CPU said.

"So who was this guy?" Justin asked.

"The blacksmith. He took care of the stables, horses and such."

"What else does your phone tell you about him?" Derrick asked.

For the remainder of the trip, CPU recounted the newspaper's tale of Yakob Heimrich. A German immigrant to the United States, he settled in Massachusetts. Krill took him on as one of his hired servants. Like all his servants, Yakob was paid very well. But before long, Krill began to suspect something about Yakob. When he returned from purchasing goods in town the amount of goods brought back started to dwindle. Yakob blamed it on increasing prices, but Krill started to think some of the funds he sent with Yakob were being pocketed, not used for purchases.

Yakob also experienced noticeable mood swings and outbursts of temper. He became more secretive and aloof, spending more time in the attic than in his own quarters. Krill did not mind Yakob using the attic; its only use was for storage. However, Yabkob's behavior grew more erratic and mysterious.

One day, while Yakob was in town, Krill's concern drove him to investigate the goings-on in the attic. His appalling discovery sickened him. Yakob had spent a small fortune on books and other items that dealt with occult practices and witchcraft. This alarmed Krill, with the Danvers witch trials still fresh in his memory. He would confront Yakob; get him to stop. Grangeville must never experience what happened in Danvers!

The disappearance of Ravenwood Estates occupants now made sense too. CPU surmised that Krill's confrontation with Yakob must have triggered the event, based on Justin's mirror experience with Krill that revealed a state of anxiety—a dreadful anticipation something monstrous was about to take place. Krill smartly made arrangements to pass down his home to someone worthy beforehand. Days later, the deed was done. Yakob must have kept Krill in bondage inside the mirror until he made known the location of his wealth. After more than three hundred years, Yakob still pressed Krill for the answer!

Living outside the mirror subjected Yakob to its terrible side effect: the necessity for life-sustaining energy. This required absorbing the life force of another human being. The alternative, to remain trapped inside the mirror, made for an abhorrent situation at best. Krill's communication with Justin did not last long, yet Krill filled in additional details as long as he was able. Holding himself together in a recognizable form took a lot out of him.

"I guess Craven *is* innocent!" Derrick said. "Now we just need to look for a three-hundred-year old ghost!"

"Or not a ghost, according to Krill," Justin corrected. "Stealing the life force gives him substance."

"Still, who is this Yakob?" CPU asked. "I mean, who is he passing himself off as today?"

"We don't even know anyone with a German accent!" Derrick added.

Justin multitasked, watched the road and mentally examined the facts. Even with so much more to go on other questions arose. They knew *what* the killer was. They just didn't know *who* the killer was!

CPU began to see Krill in a new light. Being trapped in a mirror must have changed him. Yakob's deceit could have given rise to Krill the dour old curmudgeon. At heart, Krill was actually a generous benefactor. Once the rumor mill got into full swing, Krill became a marked man waging a battle on two fronts: The townspeople and a despicable servant. CPU would not be surprised if Yakob started rumors calling his employer an 'angry hermit.'

All this thinking made Derrick hungry.

Krill told them the way to stop Yakob: break the mirror. But there was more to it. Yakob must be forced back inside the mirror seconds *before* it was destroyed. Krill would be destroyed as well. But having made peace with his Maker, he was more than ready to go home after three centuries in bondage.

Krill did not produce an identifiable image of Yakob during his encounter with Justin. Upon speculation, a blacksmith would be shorter, have a lower center of gravity to preserve his back. That's all they had to go on. He might have a German accent or may disguise it with perfect English. This meant they had to track him down somehow. Being a sorcerer could make this more difficult. Justin had no idea what impact such powers might have on his angelic abilities.

"You would think people would be smarter these days," CPU said. "You know kids, do not talk to strangers."

"Maybe he put a spell on them," Derrick surmised. "Besides his victims were older teens, not little kids."

"Well, we now know the why and how he did it," Justin said. "And maybe he wasn't so much a stranger after all, but a familiar face!"

"Who'd have thought a mirror could be a murder weapon?" Derrick said.

From the back seat CPU posed the question, "Justin, you said Craven was innocent. But right after his escape from jail another kid was killed. Is Craven this Yakob guy?"

"I think Craven is being set up," Justin said. "I know it's just my gut instinct and nothing supernatural, I just feel strongly about it."

"Yakob is setting him up?" Derrick asked. "How?"

"I'm betting Craven is his prisoner somewhere—being kept out of sight while Yakob takes more lives," Justin explained.

"Once Yakob gets what he wants, Craven gets released and arrested. This is his plan?" CPU asked.

"That's my guess," Justin said.

"You gonna let Detective Selden in on this?" Derrick asked.

"Soon," Justin answered. "Whether he'll take it well, I don't know. He's still not too keen about supernatural stuff!"

****

With Thanksgiving only three days away, Justin went out to do some errands for his mom, who busied herself at home with preparations for the holiday. A seasonal chill frosted the air as people, bundled in heavy coats, conversed back and forth. The morning sun offered as much warmth as it could, but holiday spirits were high so no one complained of the bite in the air.

When and how to inform Tom of their new information dominated Justin's thoughts today. His uncertainty centered on Tom's own approach-avoidance ambivalence accepting Justin's capabilities. It had to be soon. Based on his history, it would not be long before the serial killer required another dose of energizing life force.

Trying to focus on the errands at hand, Justin was pleasantly surprised to run into Beverly, also in preparation mode for Thanksgiving. She understood Tom; Justin would ask her how to approach him. Little did he know, Beverly had invited Tom over for Thanksgiving dinner.

"Neither one of us has family in the area," she explained.

"My family could have invited you," he replied, although the thought never occurred to him until now.

"Next year—we'll shoot for next time," Beverly said. "What's on your mind? You look like something's pressing on your brain."

She knew him very well too. He only hoped she didn't sense that bit of jealousy welling up inside him.

"Something's happened," he began. "I don't know how Tom will take it, but I need to get this information to him ASAP!"

Sensing this was going to be serious, Beverly suggested they pay for their items, find their cars, and meet in the parking lot. It turns out they parked next to each other in the Walmart lot. Justin threw his items into his car and took a front seat in Beverly's. They could sit and talk more comfortably in her roomier sedan.

He poured out his entire theory to her—all the events as he believed they happened. He didn't leave out any of the evidence, including his earlier theory of the killer's identity, now defunct. Justin's sleuthing abilities impressed her as she listened intently. Fletcher Byrd, the latest victim, stole a car, went for a joy ride, and wound up hiding the car in the woods near the mansion. Fletcher must have been in the attic, his cigarettes being found by the attic door. The part about retrieving Derrick's phone, the thing that happened next, floored Beverly.

"Josiah Krill—*spoke* to you?"

"Not in so many words," Justin said. "I sensed him and did some lip reading."

"That's incredible! Trapped in a mirror for three hundred years!"

"We have to find Yakob Heimrich!" Justin said.

"It's the mirror—right?" Beverly asked. "You said he uses it to—what, suck out the victim's life force?"

"Which is why they look the way they do."

"Your original hunch put Jake Henrycks as the killer?" she asked.

"Seems absurd—an upper-level detective on a killing spree!" Justin said.

Her face paled.

"Well, wait a moment. You found a partial zip tie with his prints, plus Henrycks followed right behind Fletcher Tuesday night?"

Her sudden, powerful discomfort forced itself upon Justin who wasn't even trying to read her. "Yes—why? I could place Henrycks and Fletcher at the mini mart that night. Is something wrong?"

"My family history goes back to Germany. Heimrich is the German surname for Henry. Yakob is German for Jacob!"

Justin started to put it together. "Jacob Henry?"

Beverly looked at Justin, her eyes narrowed. "Jake is a nickname for Jacob!" she explained. "Jake Henry—or another variant, Henrycks!"

"My theory about Henrycks could be correct after all?"

"And we need to move forward carefully!" Beverly warned.

Her explanation made him a little sick to his stomach this time. It was real. Henrycks' entire identity must be a forgery, using sorcery to create for himself a history. He was crafty, devious; did he suspect anyone was on to him?

"Justin, I better go with you when you talk to Tom," Beverly said.

Hearing she would be there to back him up eased his stomach discomfort some. She called Tom on her cell to check his availability then made room in her schedule for later in the afternoon. She declined to offer him any details over the phone, only to say it was something vital to the case he was currently working on.

Justin thanked her as he got into his own car. Signaling 'Goodbye,' they headed in opposite directions towards their respective homes.

****

Derrick arrived at Justin's house all out of breath. He explained he ran the entire way. In the urgency of this sudden, new situation he forgot he owned a car, bicycle, and motorcycle.

"Yesterday, CPU made plans to come over today," Derrick said catching his breath. "I haven't seen him!"

Justin motioned for his friend to come inside. "Maybe he's on his way now."

"There's more: his mom says his bed wasn't slept in! She's frantic!" Derrick said.

Justin called Beverly for advice. She encouraged him to take some time to look for CPU. She would go alone to prepare Tom for their new evidence and try to meet up with him later.

"We should try the mansion first," Justin said.

"You got any weapons?" Derrick asked.

"Just myself," Justin answered. "But grab my baseball bat if you want. I'll get some flashlights."

Tensions were high as the Honda pulled off Route 51 and made its way to the end of the dirt road. Fortunately, it was still daylight. The interior of the house would be dark enough. From their vantage point no discernible activity presented itself, no glowing lights appeared in the third floor windows. So far, so good, but they'd have to go inside to be certain.

Once inside they listened carefully for sounds other than the constant dripping of water from the ceiling. Crickets seemed awfully loud this time, Justin wished they'd be still for once. No human—or inhuman—sounds could be heard. Justin motioned to Derrick to follow him upstairs. At the top they listened carefully. Nothing.

Making their way down the familiar hallway, they cautiously checked each room. They swept each room with their flashlights. Again nothing.

When they reached the attic stairs and made their way up Justin had a thought. Once in the attic, he stood before the mirror and called out Krill's name. When nothing happened he tried once more. A light began to shimmer in the mirror accompanied by deep, rumbling sounds.

"Justin, he's coming!" Derrick shouted.

Blackness swelled, darted forward. In a moment, Krill's countenance appeared above the cloud. Though he'd seen it before, the frightening image still took some getting used to.

Calling in a loud voice, Justin began cautiously. "Mr. Krill, If you can understand me, I need your help."

The anguish in Krill's face almost seemed to say "What now? Why are you still here?" Without waiting, Justin asked his question.

"We need to find our friend! Where might Yakob hide someone?" Justin asked.

At first, image of Krill only formed an impression in Justin's mind: Yakob cannot stray far from the mirror for any great length of time.

Justin tried again. "Are there any other buildings on the estate grounds he might hide?"

Krill's mouth suddenly formed the word 'mausoleum.' Justin could feel Krill interred his wife there; a deep sadness accompanied the word. His cloudy image now dissipated into thousands of tiny, sparkling lights and he was gone.

Justin and Derrick made their way outside, appreciating the little bit of extra light that made it through the trees. Fortunately, these dark woods afforded a bit more comfort and light than the gloomy attic. Justin reached for his cell phone, which really shone brightly by comparison.

"It's here, on my phone." Justin, his eyes adjusting to the phone's brightness, scanned a piece of information recorded from the library. What appeared to be a mausoleum stood a couple hundred yards to the northwest. A compass app on his phone showed them the way.

"This place is like a jungle," Derrick complained.

"It's not much farther," Justin assured him.

After several minutes of trudging through the woods a large, one-story building finally appeared. Six ornate columns, tangled in vines, straddled the entrance—three on each side of a heavy wrought-iron door. Elaborate angelic figures were carved into the stone along each side of the mausoleum. It looked big enough to inter a dozen individuals, as if Krill intended to offer it as a final resting place for all of his servants.

The boys entered and pushed the heavy iron gate, which moaned under its own weight, aside. There were no windows, so flashlights quickly emerged from their backpacks to light the interior.

Angelic senses suddenly kicked in. "Someone has been here," Justin said.

"Yakob?" Derrick asked.

Justin ignored the question for the moment, his senses still working. "No cobwebs—in the entrance or over here!"

He was right. They shone their lights around the interior. Several stone sarcophagi lay in rows along the floor. Intricately carved heavenly symbols appeared on the sides and lids. A pattern of disturbed cobwebs made it obvious each lid had been moved to search inside for something, then put back. A stone bench occupied the middle of each wall except one. The floor plan was shaped like an 'L', with the upper portion of the 'L' containing the sarcophagi. The lower portion, at the rear of the mausoleum, was empty except for a small statue standing next to a bench.

"Looks expensive," Derrick remarked.

"Yeah...speaking of cobwebs, notice that?" Justin asked. "Every bench is covered in cobwebs, but not that one back there."

Justin aimed his light onto each bench around the room, then back to the one sitting by itself. Derrick went back for a closer look. He saw an arc scratched in the stone floor to the left of the bench, an arc formed in the dust. The arc swung toward the bench, stopping about a foot in front of it. He pounded the wall with his fist. It was solid.

"Justin, look at this!"

Justin examined the floor. He ran his flashlight up and down the wall. In the light he could see a nearly imperceptibly fine seam running from the floor to about halfway to the ceiling. "There must be a room on the other side of this wall."

"OK, but how do we get inside?" Derrick asked.

Justin eyed the statue nearby. It didn't budge when he tried to turn it on its base.

"I'm getting tired; I need to sit down," Derrick said. He dropped himself down on the bench. The seat wobbled. "This bench is loose!"

"Let's see, get up!" Derrick stood and Justin grabbed the front edge of the bench and pulled up. It made an audible 'click.'

Derrick jumped. The wall next to the bench slowly opened towards them with a loud, grinding noise of stone against stone. "The wall's moving!"

One foot of open, solid stone wall presented them with a gaping black hole—an inner room. They aimed their flashlights inside and peeked in. It took them a moment to understand what it was they saw. A chair in the center of the small room had something tied to it.

"It's Doctor Craven!" Derrick cried.

Craven did not move; he was out cold. Derrick used the knife on the Gerber tool he carried with him to cut the restraints. When released, Craven slumped off the chair onto the floor.

"We need to get him to a hospital!" Justin said.

"But what about CPU?" Derrick reminded him.

"At least we know he's not here…"

"Not yet anyway!" Derrick interrupted.

"Right. But we can't leave the doctor here!" Justin said.

They decided to make the trip to the hospital. It was not far and on the way Derrick called home in case CPU did finally show up. He had not. Justin informed Derrick he suddenly remembered Beverly was waiting for him at police headquarters. Derrick, although a little anxious to keep searching for his friend, saw some wisdom in staying with Craven at the hospital. Craven might be able to tell him Henrycks' or CPU's whereabouts. He'd wait there until Justin returned from his meeting with Selden.

They pulled up to the Emergency Entrance, the Honda's tires screeching to a stop. An ER attendant rushed outside, met Derrick, and helped him get Craven inside. Derrick filled him in on as much as he knew of the man's condition. When he gave the 'thumbs up,' Justin drove off.

Chapter 15

Charles Underwood's eyes scanned his unfamiliar surroundings. The large, open area, perhaps a warehouse or factory, had long since been abandoned. Levered windows ran the entire length of two of the walls, at least thirty feet above the floor. Some windows were open, some shattered, most were closed. Blackness filled the windows telling him it must be late in the day. Exposed plumbing, pipes and valves, ran from floor to ceiling at various points around the room. CPU, seated on the bare, concrete floor, zip-tied to one of those pipes, made a failed effort to free himself.

The vast room was cold, in spite of his heavy parka. Fortunately, he did not have to experience the minus five degree wind-chill of the outdoors. His rear end was sore and cold from half-sitting, half-laying down on the bare floor. His wrists, likewise, were equally tender from the awkward position they were tied against the pipes. Except for an occasional rattle of windows against the chilling gusts of wind, the place was exceedingly quiet.

The awful smelling gas being sprayed in his face was the last thing CPU remembered. Now, awake for what felt like two hours, his captor was nowhere to be seen. He spent most of this time praying, hoping someone was looking for him.

His foggy memory slowly returned allowing him to rehash the events leading up to his capture.

Justin had just dropped him off at the end of his street, a few houses down from his own. A moment later, an unmarked police car pulled up alongside him. Detective Henrycks rolled down the passenger window and called over to him.

"Charles! Do you have a few minutes? I have a few further questions for you."

"It's getting late. Let me go tell my mom first," CPU answered.

Henrycks stopped the car in the middle of the street, got out, went around to the rear passenger-side door and opened it. "This will only take two minutes, Promise!" he said.

CPU acquiesced and got into the back seat of the car. Henrycks closed the door, got back into the driver's seat and drove off.

"Where are we going?" CPU asked.

"Someplace where you'll be safe," Henrycks said.

"Safe? From what?"

Henrycks shot a quick glance into the rear view mirror. A twisted smile crossed his face. It gave CPU the chills. "Safe from your friends, of course!" Henrycks said. "Especially Justin!"

An unbelievable conversation ensued. Henrycks, for whatever reason, had developed a fear of Justin. He sensed a strength in the boy possessed by no other. Henrycks words made little sense to CPU. Why would an Angel Falls detective fear Justin or want to separate him from his friends? The question sent his mind into overdrive, with computer-like speed, to sort through tons of data. Then it hit him. A cold shockwave ran from his chest, outward, numbing CPU's arms and legs.

Eyes wide, mouth agape, he finally got the words out, "You...You're Yakob Heimrich!"

Henrycks, or Heimrich, let out a loud sigh, his words suddenly exhibiting a heavy German accent, "Ah, see? This is all because of the dangerous company you keep!"

****

Justin arrived at police headquarters, made his way to Tom Selden's office, whereupon he found Beverly in the middle of a heated conversation with the detective. It wouldn't be easy to convince Tom his lead detective was not who he thought he was. By the look and sound of things, having the news come from Beverly did not soften the blow. Not only did Justin hear Tom use Beverly's full name again, he added her surname as well. He was beyond upset!

"Beverly Heartstone, my lead detective is not your serial killer!" Tom shouted. "You and Justin need to have your heads examined!"

"Where is Detective Henrycks now?" she shouted back.

Tom shot out of his chair, shoved it back under his desk, and paced back and forth. "Looking for Craven, I suppose!"

"You *suppose*?" Beverly's tone was critical. "When did he last check in?"

Tom stopped pacing. He looked at his watch. He stared at the ceiling for several seconds, as if waiting for it to fall down on him. He looked back at his watch. He grabbed his chair, yanked it out from under his desk and dropped himself back down into it, massaging his eyes with his palms.

Then he slammed both fists down onto his desk and growled, "Great! Just great!"

"Tom, what is it?" Beverly asked.

"It's not like him," Tom said, "It's been three hours without checking in!"

Justin used this moment to cautiously make his presence known. He took the seat next to Beverly's. "Derrick and I found Doctor Craven!"

Tom removed his hands from his face and looked at Justin through blurred eyes. "*You* found him—where?"

"CPU is missing, so Derrick and I went looking for him," Justin began. "We learned of a mausoleum behind the mansion. That's where we first looked for CPU. We found the doctor instead."

Tom looked shell shocked. "Whatever made you go to a mausoleum?"

Ignoring his question, Justin continued, "He was unconscious, bound to a chair in a hidden room for what looks like several days."

Beverly intervened, "Several days! Looks like this takes Craven off the prime suspect list!"

"So, where is Craven now?" Tom asked.

"Derrick is staying with him in the hospital. We hope you can get some answers out of him when he's in better shape."

"Justin, you said your friend is missing?" Beverly asked.

"He never came home last night. No one knows where he is." Justin said.

Tom, a little calmer now, wanted answers. "I'll ask again, why the mausoleum?"

"Based on other evidence, the abandoned mansion is the perfect hiding place."

"But you said 'mausoleum.'"

"When we found the mansion empty, we learned about the mausoleum," Justin said.

"How? What's your source?" Tom asked. He now seemed prepared to listen.

Justin shifted nervously in his chair. "It's how we learned about Yakob Heimrich."

Tom's impatience matched his tone. "Right, my detective...where is all this coming from, Justin?"

"Better be prepared for the answer, Tom," Beverly said.

****

After sitting beside Brent Craven's hospital bed for an hour, Derrick began to get antsy. An intravenous line in Craven's arm delivered much needed nutrients he'd been lacking for days. Occasionally, one of the nurses would come by to check on him, take his vitals and mark his chart. The look on one nurse's face seemed to indicate he was beginning to come around. Sure enough, after the last nurse dismissed herself, Craven groaned. He moved his head side to side and tried to lift it. Derrick got up from his chair and stood by the bed.

"Doctor, are you all right?" he asked.

Another moan. This time the patient's eyes fluttered. They looked at Derrick, blinking several times.

"You...aren't you one of the students that interviewed me?" Craven asked.

Of all the things to ask about after being abducted! Derrick forgot about their little ruse; the question caught him by surprise.

"Uh, yeah, but forget about that. Do you remember what happened to you?"

Craven closed his eyes momentarily in thought. "How long have I been here?"

"You've been here for an hour, but were missing for a few days," Derrick answered. "Can you remember anything?"

"Yes. The awful odor of chloroform—not much else."

"Think hard; you have to remember something!" Derrick urged.

Craven was silent for several minutes, intermittently groaning as he rubbed his forehead. A momentary look of discomfort crossed his face, then he looked at Derrick.

"Tied to a chair—yes, it was dark—and a voice!" Craven said.

"Did you see who it was; could you recognize the voice?"

"The voice—no. His voice was deep, muffled—maybe German. The darkness played tricks on my eyes, but all I could make out was something—a darker silhouette against the far wall."

"Describe it," Derrick said.

"Fairly large, but not tall. It moved in the shadows the whole time."

"Do you remember being moved to another location during your captivity?" Derrick asked.

"Moved? I don't know. Most of it's a hazy blur."

Derrick thanked the doctor and excused himself. Once out in the waiting room he made a quick call home, then called Justin.

When Justin answered Derrick asked, "Where are you?"

"Still with Tom, what's up?"

"Craven woke up. His captor, what he can remember of the incident, sounds like our Henrycks," Derrick said. "Short and large, probably German."

"That's not much to go on. Did he remember where he was kept?"

"Unfortunately, no," Derrick said.

"Thanks, Derrick. I'll pass this on to Detective Selden, for whatever it's worth. I'll finish up here. See you in twenty minutes."

"That's OK. Mom is picking me up," Derrick said. "Then I'm going out to find CPU myself."

"Come by the station. I want to go with you," Justin suggested. "There's strength in numbers. We need to be careful!"

****

Somewhere CPU heard a door slam, followed by the sound of shoes advancing along the concrete floor. He thought if Justin could pick up a spiritual vibe, he'd scream out Justin's name as loud as he could. Henrycks continued to approach from the other end of the building. He laughed as CPU's voice echoed Justin's name throughout the warehouse walls. When Henrycks arrived at his prisoner's feet he pulled up an old crate and sat down on it and faced him.

"What is it about your friend, Justin? You think he can hear you?" Henrycks asked.

CPU did not answer. He thought better about revealing anything about Justin to this madman.

"I sensed in him something… an empathy? Is he an empath? I've never encountered such a thing in another human being!" Henrycks told CPU. "I did not dare leave Justin alone with Doctor Craven, lest he discover his innocence!"

"What are you saying?" CPU asked.

"Just that I have certain 'gifts'," Henrycks said. "A spell I placed on the doctor blocks an empath's perceptions! Very handy when I was not present during interrogations."

"But when you were present—is it because of you Justin felt sick during those times?"

"He was too annoying to have around!" Henrycks laughed. "Asking so many questions!"

The hubris of this Henrycks, or Heimrich! It seemed to delight him to offer up details of his crimes! CPU decided he might use this to his advantage. Working through his fear, he screwed up his courage to ask more questions. It wasn't quite enough courage to drop the contractions, however. But, the more he could find out about Henrycks, the easier, he hoped, it would be to stop him.

"You didn't actually come here from Philadelphia, did you?" CPU asked him.

"I have always been in Grangeville, uh, Angel Falls."

"Grangeville? The town hasn't been called Grangeville for a few hundred years!"

"The mirror held me captive for thirty-two decades—now, at last, I am free!"

CPU remembered Justin mentioning something about this guy's odd way of thinking about the number thirty-two. "You don't look three hundred years old!" CPU said.

"My mirror keeps me young," Henrycks answered with fondness in his tone.

"The same mirror that imprisoned you?" CPU asked. "I don't understand."

A look of disgust appeared on Henrycks face. "Thirty-two." Henrycks said.

"Thirty-two?" CPU asked.

"A number—very special. It always shows up," Henrycks began. "As a novice, my attempt to use that number to protect the mirror went terribly wrong! I accidentally transferred myself inside with everyone else—for thirty-two decades!"

"And once the mirror released you, you went on a killing spree?"

"Once outside, I found myself getting weaker with each passing day. At over three-hundred-years old who wouldn't be?" Henrycks said. He chuckled. "Now the mirror is my source of energy. Fortunately, you will be the last life I will require to gain my total freedom."

CPU picked up on several things as he listened. Not only is Henrycks living on borrowed time, he also caught that last remark about being Henrycks' last victim. But most importantly, Henrycks revealed a weakness, a possible way to stop him.

"What did you mean, 'protect the mirror?'" CPU asked.

"I think that's enough questions for now, young Charles," Henrycks quickly replied. "We must be on our way!"

"Where are we going?"

Henrycks approached CPU to lift him off the floor. "Why to the mansion, of course!"

Chapter 16

Derrick and Justin got together to consider CPU's whereabouts. Tom Selden put another detective on the case as well. He also gave Justin his direct cell number in case they ran into any trouble. Tom finally accepted, with a few minor reservations, the evidence he and Derrick passed along to him. Tom immediately set in motion a BOLO for Henrycks. Beverly returned to the Tribune to work up a story—what kind of story, she wasn't yet certain.

"What if we use 'Fone Finder' to look for CPU? Derrick suddenly asked.

"Henrycks probably got rid of his phone," Justin said.

"Well, all we're doin' now is riding around aimlessly—it couldn't hurt!" Derrick said.

Derrick did not have the app, so he immediately downloaded it, installed it, and turned it on. Entering CPU's number did absolutely nothing.

"I guess you're right; Henrycks got rid of the phone," Derrick groaned.

"Let's keep driving—see what happens," Justin said.

They decided to take 51 north. About fifteen miles from the mansion road Derrick's phone started beeping. 'Fone Finder' suddenly became active and was telling them CPU's phone was two miles ahead.

"I gotta get a new phone with better coverage," Derrick said.

The signal sent them to a gravel path right off 51 with a chain running across it. The path was only wide enough to accommodate one vehicle at a time. An unlocked padlock secured one end of the chain to a steel post. The chain was welded to another post at the opposite side of the path. Tall, thick swamp grass ran along the sides of the pathway, which disappeared deep into a heavily wooded area.

"It's in here—wherever 'here' is," Derrick said.

"You want to do the honors?" Justin asked.

Derrick looked over at him "Huh?"

"Release the chain so we can get in!" Justin said.

Derrick complied, hopped out of the car, released the chain and hopped back into the car. The surrounding area was desolate, with no buildings in sight, just tall grass and trees. The red dot representing CPU's phone continued to beep and blink.

"The road has to curve right up ahead if we're gonna stay on course," Derrick noted.

Sure enough, a right-hand bend in the road appeared. Moments later, the road took a turn to the left. It was at that point they noticed a large warehouse further ahead. It looked deserted. Weeds broke through cracks everywhere in the surface of the parking lot.

"It has to be in there," Derrick said.

Justin pulled up to the nearest entrance, where someone had left a door propped open with a cinder block and parked the Honda. Entering, they walked down a hallway past several abandoned offices. At the end of one hallway a door opened up into a vast open area.

Derrick pointed to the left. "His phone is over that way."

About forty feet further they made a horrific discovery: a set of those familiar zip ties hung loosely from a pipe.

Derrick examined the zip tie. "Is that blood?"

"He must have struggled. Those things give nasty cuts!" Justin said.

"There's something over there," Derrick said. He picked up a folded cloth from the floor, next to a crate. He gave the cloth the once over and held it up to his nose.

"Phew! What a stink!"

The pungent odor was like a punch between the eyes. The cloth fell from his hands and Derrick teetered forward, then backward. To keep from falling he dropped himself onto a nearby crate. He remained there, sitting still until the dizziness passed.

"What happened? Are you OK?" Justin asked.

"It's chloroform!" Derrick said. "The odor is still strong which means it hasn't all evaporated yet—Henrycks left with CPU recently!"

"He must be getting weak," Justin said. "He'll need the mirror!"

The Honda's engine roared as they charged off toward the mansion about four miles from their current location. Derrick called Detective Selden.

"Tell him to meet us at the end of the service road—do not go into the mansion until we get there!" Justin instructed.

"You have a plan?" Derrick asked as he dialed Tom's number.

"To save our friend!" Justin said. "And permanently rid Angel Falls of this menace!"

****

"Beverly here."

"Bev, it's Tom." The urgency in Tom's voice made Beverly sit upright and pay special attention. "You have a police scanner in your office, don't you?" Tom asked.

"Yes. Tom, what's the matter?"

"The bizarre is about to hit the fan!" Tom said. "I'm off to the mansion to meet Justin; keep your ears open for any distress calls!"

"Please explain!" Beverly urged.

"I don't want to become shredded Styrofoam or locked up inside some mirror!"

"Justin found Henrycks?"

"And CPU. If Justin knows what he's doing, we'll prevent another death!"

"Is there anything else I can do?" Beverly asked.

"I'd ask you to pray, but you don't roll that way," Tom said.

"Be careful, Tom! And I do so pray!" Beverly objected. "And you can trust Justin!"

****

CPU lay on the attic floor in front of the mirror, unconscious. Henrycks avoided standing in front of the mirror. He always kept off to the side of the room in the shadows. Right now he occupied himself with a large book of spells, looking for something to thwart intruders. This last hope of deliverance from the mirror excited him but also made him very anxious. Everything must go as planned!

The mirror, his salvation, was also his worst fear. It scared him to death. Absorbing the entire Krill household was another error in the newbie sorcerer's judgement. He was able to grow in strength by killing off Krill's staff, one at a time. He kept Krill for his knowledge of the treasure. Once outside the mirror he required a constant source of new energy. One last victim was all he needed to be totally and finally free. His confidence began to grow when his blood turned cold. A voice called to him from the mirror. It was a voice he knew all too well. A voice he alone could hear. A voice he hated. Josiah Krill condemned his practice of the occult.

"I'll be rid of you soon, Krill!" Henrycks hollered at the voice in the mirror. He laughed maniacally, "All that will be left of you is dust!"

"Prayer trumps sorcery every time, Yakob!" He heard Krill say.

"I succeeded in ruining your reputation, old man!" Henrycks replied. "You will be just a sad footnote in history!"

"You will not harm that young man!" came the voice from the mirror.

"Tell you what. Point me to your treasure and I will spare the boy!" he lied.

The mirror went silent, but Henrycks knew he would soon possess the mansion and all its riches! He moved across the room, past the mirror, to wake CPU. Charles, groggy at first, finally stood.

Henrycks had him face the mirror, then stood far off into the shadows to watch.

****

Tom recognized Henrycks unmarked vehicle back near Route 51. He despised the unpleasant duty before him, but he knew now what had to be done. Tom, Justin, and Derrick hid behind the trees just beyond the mansion's front porch. From their vantage point they would be able to see any activity through the windows.

"It will happen up there," Justin said pointing to the blacked-out attic window high above them. "Be sure to remain silent once we're inside. Follow me up the attic stairs. Stay close, Tom, but do not enter the attic—just observe from the top stair until I signal you in. Derrick, I need you at the other end of the room, by the table."

"You'll be doing your 'thing'?" Derrick asked. "He won't see me?"

"He won't see any of us; leave that to me!" Justin said.

"We'd better get going!" Tom said.

Approaching the building, they stopped at the broken window and peered inside. It was dark, no movement detected, so they climbed inside. Tom was amazed at how well the furnishings were preserved, how ornate the woodwork was. He never realized such a place existed, although he remembered Beverly's stories of similar places still located elsewhere in Angel Falls.

Avoiding spiders, a raccoon, and vines hanging from the ceiling, the three made their way to the stairway. In hushed tones, Justin warned Tom about the creepy portrait at the top of the stairs. He also whispered to him to tread carefully due to the slippery mossy coating on some of the steps. Tom understood, grateful for the advanced warning. They successfully made it to the second floor landing. Now it was time for Justin to take over as he motioned for Tom and Derrick to advance to the end of the hall. They stayed close, remaining absolutely quiet, and climbed the stairs to the attic. They could hear Henrycks' voice as they approached.

****

"This won't hurt a bit," Henrycks lied to CPU.

"Justin!" CPU cried out, unable to move.

Henrycks, or Heimrich, laughed. "There *is* something about this Justin! What is it?"

"You'll find out!" CPU promised.

"It will be too late for you, I'm afraid!" Henrycks replied. "There is no one around to hear your calls for help!"

His confidence growing, Henrycks rambled on about how he first tried to frame Jeb Wechsler for the killings. The old man got too nosey about his grandson. He needed to be removed. Unfortunately, the hair taken from his laptop belonged to CPU, not Brian's grandfather. It was a small wrench in the works, but once he turned his attention toward Craven everything fell into place.

"Until your friends found where I hid the doctor!" Henrycks fumed. "But no matter. Once finished here, no one can stop me!"

Henrycks continued his musing:

"Used a bit of sorcery to sneak Craven out of jail. I'd hide him away—it was a bit of genius—as soon as he was freed, the deaths would start again! Between that and being caught trying to harm his old patient, he looked *so* guilty!"

CPU stood, motionless and trance-like, unable to move. He barely heard what Henrycks went on about. Suddenly, a blue glow slowly emanated from within the mirror. It's rays extended outward, reaching for the young boy. Henrycks closed his eyes, enjoying the moment, when he felt a sudden uneasiness. A fleeting, unusual sensation pressed against his mind. The room seemed to turn. Believing it was due to the excitement, he watched the blue glow expand with anticipation. Then he heard a familiar voice.

"Now, Tom!" Justin shouted.

Henrycks heard Justin's voice, blinked, swooned—looked around. CPU no longer stood in front of the mirror! *He* was standing where CPU had been!

"What trickery is this!?" Henrycks growled, his head swooning.

Behind his image in the mirror Henrycks saw Tom. Instantly, his fellow police officer lunged at him from behind! Henrycks attempted to turn to stop him, but Tom shoved Henrycks hard, causing him to lose his balance. When Henrycks fell backwards towards the mirror he caught a split second glimpse of CPU—standing over by the doorway next to Justin!

Henrycks howled. He screamed, he felt his body being torn from one dimension into another! Arms flailing, legs kicking, the blue light faded as the mirror swallowed him!

"Derrick, *now*—before he can escape!" Justin shouted.

Tom quickly moved away from the mirror. Derrick reached for the world globe on the table in the middle of the room. He hoisted the heavy object over his right shoulder with a grunt and hurled it like a shot-put with all his might. The impact with the mirror exploded into hundreds of shards of glass and ceramic flying everywhere!

As did thousands of gold coins from inside the globe when it burst open!

Derrick ran over to pick up as many coins as he could. To his horror the coins started slowly to slide across the floor towards the mirror. Then the coins rose from the floor, picked up speed, and flew inside the mirror. Now charts on the table next to him rose into the air to be swiftly sucked up into the mirror. More objects in the room became caught up in a loud, violent whirlwind pulling everything in its grasp into the mirror!

"Derrick, everyone, get out!" Justin yelled.

Derrick did not waste time picking up any more gold. He flew out the door following Tom, CPU, and Justin. They sprinted down the hall, bounding down two stairs at a time, and climbed out the front window. Overhead, a thundering locomotive of noise from splitting wooden beams and shattering glass offended their ears. Justin and the others found a safe distance away from the mansion. In amazement they watched as the attic roof collapsed, pulled into the mirror along with the walls. Floorboards ripped up, flying into the mirror. Soon other parts of the mansion imploded in upon itself, sucked into the mirror. Second floor, first floor, all pulled inward until ending in an implosion of blinding white light.

The house was gone; the mirror vanished. Nothing but a shallow, blackened mansion-shaped crater remained where once a stone mansion stood.

"CPU, are you OK?" Derrick asked his friend.

"Eyes and ears still adjusting, but great otherwise!" CPU replied.

"What about you, Tom?" Justin asked.

Tom looked around. He appeared a bit shaken; it took a moment for him to respond.

"That was amazing!" he shouted.

"Welcome to Justin's world," Derrick said.

Chapter 17

On this beautiful November day, only one day before Thanksgiving, Justin, Derrick, CPU, Tom, and Beverly took their seats in a large, circular booth at Falls Diner. Lunch was on Tom, who was glad to be alive! Justin looked around at the other patrons in the diner. None of them realized the enormity of what occurred the day before. A good thing it was; town-wide panic does not look pretty!

Today's story in the Trib, written by Beverly, told of the 'capture' of the Angel Falls serial killer. Shockwaves rippled through Angel Falls upon learning the guilty party was their new police detective. Tom dealt with the paperwork of the case, making sure to cover up any 'otherworldly' information. He also dealt with some of the backlash the news created, which protested the vetting process of Henrycks. He should have been vetted more thoroughly!

The news also reported Henrycks would be shipped off to a maximum security prison in another part of the country. Meanwhile, CPU became a celebrity at school having escaped the clutches of the killer. The mansion was never mentioned in the news; still remaining unknown to the general public.

"It's still hard to believe, Bev!" Tom said as their drinks were served. "If I hadn't seen it with my own eyes…. You should have been there!"

"No thanks! I had enough excitement with our last encounter with evil!" she said.

Tom continued. "Justin had Henrycks all confused—he actually never saw us coming!"

"I told you," Beverly replied. "He's our perfect weapon against this kind of otherworldly nonsense!"

As soon as their meals arrived, CPU started right in on his hamburger. He hadn't eaten since yesterday's traumatic event. He was famished.

"Henrycks confessed to everything—he thought no one else was around to hear him!" Tom said. "While we were standing right next to him!"

"Doctor Craven is certainly happy to be free and clear," Justin said before taking a bite out of his honey mustard chicken wrap.

Justin glanced over at his friend who barely touched his lunch. Avoiding food was very unusual for Derrick. "Derrick, what's wrong?"

"I was only able to grab three gold coins," he said.

"Just be glad the mirror did not *grab you*!" CPU said.

Beverly guzzled down her iced tea. "Man, I was thirsty!" she said. "Derrick, it was still nice of you to give CPU and Justin each a coin!" She flagged down their waiter, "Can I have another iced tea, please!"

Tom finished his Reuben and Coke. "Justin, I apologize for the difficult time I gave you; you really came through!"

Justin cleared his throat. "Likewise. I know *I* can be a handful at times."

"It's going to take me a while to fully wrap my head around all this!" Tom confessed.

Beverly smiled. "If I can get used to it, I'm sure you will, Tom!"

"I have to admit," Justin cut in, "Even I'm still trying to 'wrap my head around it' as you say."

"We just need a break," Derrick added. "Two major catastrophes in just three months is too heavy to handle!"

"I can agree to that!" Beverly said finishing her second iced tea.

Tom raised his hand, "Waitress, the check, please!"

****

"Christmas is only two weeks away!" CPU said with his usual excitement.

"What are you getting me?" Derrick asked.

"New socks, your feet stink!" CPU laughed.

"Maybe you *should* put your shoes back on, Derrick," Justin said.

"Hey, I meant to tell you guys—I went to the library yesterday," CPU said. "I found this book on ancient artifacts."

"More occultist stuff, huh? You gotta stay away from that stuff, Chuck!" Derrick warned.

"Not at all, just myths and legends," CPU replied. "Kind of interesting!"

"Sort of like 'Ripley's Believe It Or Not'," Justin said.

"Something like that," CPU said. "But there was a drawing of a ring—it looked exactly like that one Doctor Craven wore!"

"Exactly? As ugly as the doctor's?" Derrick asked.

"Here, look…." CPU handed them the book.

Derrick read the caption. "A Longevity Ring. Only a few are supposed to exist—it's ugly all right!"

Justin changed the subject. "Hey, whose up for a movie?"

A movie sounded like just the thing to take their minds off recent events. Longevity rings sounded too much like sorcery to consider it any further! With a new comedy playing at the theater in town, everyone rushed to put on their coats and head for the Honda.

"Shotgun!" Derrick called.

****

Doctor Brent Craven went out to survey what, if anything, remained of the mansion. With the holiday over, the weather began to grow colder as winter approached. Craven pulled the zipper of his coat higher to ward off a sudden wind chill. It shocked him to see the mansion-sized crater was all that remained of the once magnificent stone building.

He considered removing some of the trees and building a log cabin, then laughed at the thought. No, another mansion, better than the first, is what he'd build. He would, however, remove specific trees if only to let more light into the estate. He could easily afford the massive undertaking; money was not an issue for him. It would also be necessary to repair damage to the estate's wall and put in a new gate.

Fortunately, the mausoleum still stood! Craven found relief from the wind as he made his way inside. He turned on a battery-operated lantern he carried with him and went directly to the stone bench in back of the mausoleum. He raised and lowered the seat on the stone bench. Immediately, the wall swung open. Craven went into the smaller room, talking softly to himself.

"Foolish Yakob, If only you had known how close you were!" he said aloud to himself.

Putting the lantern on the floor where Henrycks had held him captive, Craven approached a two-foot statue, an angel standing upon a four-foot pedestal in the corner of the room. He grabbed the statue with both hands, giving it a one-quarter turn clockwise on its pedestal. It turned with some difficulty after three hundred years of remaining motionless. It finally turned nonetheless, then stopped with a click. With a groan, another wall inside the inner room opened. Craven picked up the lantern to take a look inside.

Standing before all of Krill's wealth, Craven smiled widely. This was all legally his, thanks to Josiah Krill, his friend and benefactor. Aiming his light elsewhere, paintings by Rubens, El Greco, and Titian leaned against the walls. A vase from the Ming Dynasty, the First Folio collection of Shakespeare, plus other rare works presented themselves under the lantern's light. Krill had traveled the world before settling in Massachusetts, collecting rare and valuable items as he went. He even earned forty pounds of gold coins—payment in return for a favor performed for Captain William Kidd.

Craven reached into his coat pocket and gingerly pulled out a very old, worn piece of paper. He unfolded the note and read:

"My Dear Mr. Reese, There is deviltry afoot, with Heimrich at the helm. If anything happens to me, I wish for you to retain my goods and the deed to this place for your own. Keep them safe, my friend. Protect yourself. I will never forget your loyalty and kindness. Yours, Josiah Krill"

Craven folded the note and returned it to his pocket. He looked at the ring he always wore on his left hand, "Yakob, I too had my own source of magic!"

Craven slowly removed the ring. It actually felt good to be relieved of it after three hundred years! Removing it meant he no longer had to change locations every few years to avoid suspicion. If he stayed in one place too long, neighbors would notice that he never aged. Now it was time to grow old naturally, something he, with all his wealth, could look forward to. Immortality can be very tiresome!

W.A. Holmes

Epilogue

In three months construction on the new mansion commences. Trees will be cleared, the wall repaired, with major landscaping to begin. The new home of Doctor Brent Craven will take three months to complete. It promises to be more magnificent than its predecessor. One construction worker surveying the area will come across something glistening in the sunlight as it breaks through the trees. In the middle of the dark crater where once stood the old domicile he will find four shiny coins: one quarter, a nickel, and two pennies. How odd, he will think, to find thirty-two cents out in the middle of nowhere! Even odder: all the coins are decades old, yet each one is in perfect, mint condition!

THE END